Mermaid Stories

Also available from Macmillan Children's Books

Princess Stories
Chosen by Anna Wilson

Fairy Stories
Chosen by Anna Wilson

Ballerina Stories
Chosen by Emma Young

Christmas Stories
Chosen by Gaby Morgan

Pirate Stories
Chosen by Emma Young

Mermaid Stories

Chosen by Emma Young

Illustrated by Lara Jones

MACMILLAN CHILDREN'S BOOKS

For my parents

First published 2008 by Macmillan Children's Books
a division of Macmillan Publishers Limited
20 New Wharf Road, London N1 9RR
Basingstoke and Oxford
Associated companies throughout the world
www.panmacmillan.com

ISBN 978-0-330-45406-3

1 3 5 7 9 8 6 4 2

A CIP catalogue record for this book is available from
the British Library.

Designed by Nigel Hazle
Printed and bound in the UK by CPI Mackays, Chatham ME5 8TD

Contents

Hans Christian Andersen's
The Little Mermaid

Retold by Anna Wilson

Deep beneath the roaring waves
and storms and ships and fishing
boats lived the Mer-king. His home
was a glorious palace of pink and
orange coral, its windows sparkling
with jewels from shipwrecked
galleons, its roof tiled with shells.

1

The Mer-king shared his palace with his six daughters and their grandmother. The mermaids' mother had died when her youngest was born. It was perhaps because of this that his youngest daughter was quieter and more of a dreamer than her sisters. She was also the most beautiful of them all: there was something astonishing about her aquamarine eyes and sun-gold hair.

The sisters delighted in each other's company.

2

They especially loved to explore new areas of their father's kingdom together, and often brought back treasures from their excursions: curious items that had fallen from the cargoes of the ships that passed overhead. The Mer-king smiled indulgently when they showed him the strange objects.

'Why don't you each make a garden with your treasures?' he suggested one day.

'Maybe Mother will see our gardens – maybe she is watching

3

over us,' the little mermaid said.

Her grandmother nodded. 'We turn to foam when we leave this watery world,' she said. 'So in a way your dear mother is all around us.'

And so the little mermaid resolved to make a garden worthy of her mother. She called to her sisters to set off in search of more treasures.

Swishing through seaweed and skimming over peach-coloured coral, the mermaids came to a large wreck they had never seen before.

4

A dazzling array of precious gems littered the sand beneath their tails.

The five older mermaids hastily gathered as many of the precious jewels as they could manage, and were ready to swim back when they realized that their little sister was sitting staring into the eyes of a marble statue. It was of a man, and a handsome one – but it was still only a statue.

'Stop dreaming and help us!' the five sisters called.

'No,' said the little mermaid

5

resolutely, 'I shall take this with me.'
And she grasped the statue firmly
and tugged it free of the wreck
while her older sisters shook their
heads in bewilderment.

On their return, little mermaid
rushed to show her statue to her
father and grandmother.

'It is a prince,' her grandmother
said. 'See his crown and the pattern
on his shield?'

The little mermaid sat entranced
as her grandmother spoke of the
world above the sea. She was

fascinated by the ways of men and the ships they sailed and the strange creatures with which they lived.

'How do you know these things?' the little mermaid asked.

'When a mermaid has lived fifteen years, she may swim to the surface of the water,' her grandmother answered. 'I had my fill of these things many years ago. They are wonderful to behold at first, but a mermaid must learn that her life is beneath the waves.'

The little mermaid realized

7

excitedly that she would be fifteen the next year.

The waxing and waning of the moon dragged out the next few months with an impossible slowness. The little mermaid was itching for her fifteenth birthday, for the day she could find out about the world above.

For months the little mermaid's pretty head was swimming with

8

thoughts of scarlet sunsets, crimson clouds and beautiful birds. As her fifteenth birthday approached, she spent more and more hours gazing at her statue and wishing . . . wishing . . .

At last it was her birthday! Her grandmother brushed her hair and put a tiny crown of silver shells on her head. Her family waved and called out blessings.

The little mermaid broke through the surface and felt a strange sensation as the air brushed against

9

her skin. She gulped and coughed as she became accustomed to breathing in this unfamiliar way. But she soon forgot her discomfort as she drank in the sights she had dreamed of for so long.

After some time she spotted a galleon in full sail. She saw a colourful flag too, fluttering in the breeze. Swimming towards the ship, she gasped as she recognized the pattern on the flag — it was the same royal ensign she had seen on her statue's shield.

'My prince!' she cried.

A mermaid can swim as fast as a dolphin, and soon she was close enough to make out the figures on board. She saw her prince, and felt her heart quicken as she gazed at his face, which was even more beautiful than her statue's. She longed to call out to him. But while she had been swimming the sky above her had darkened and storm clouds had gathered. She swam on regardless, as the waves became columns of black raging fury and

11

the rain slashed her face.

Ahead of her, the prince's vessel struggled against the tempest, tossed about like a giant's plaything. Finally it gave up its fight and toppled over, splintering into matchsticks against the wrath of the waves. The little mermaid cried out as she watched the small figure of her prince flung through the air like a doll by the angry howling storm. She hurled herself at him, her only thought to save him from drowning. As she grasped his limp body, a flash of lightning lit up his face and she kissed it, her tears mingling with the seawater.

She held fiercely to the prince and swam from the wreck as the storm abated and the debris of the ship sank beneath the waves. The tempest died away and night fell as the mermaid swam to a bay near a large stone building. She sat in the shallows, holding the prince in her arms, waiting for morning, singing quietly to pass the time.

When the sun rose the sky was

13

peaceful. The little mermaid gently laid the prince on a plateau of warm rock and hid as the sound of bells filled the sweet air and seagulls called out to one another. It was not long before someone saw the body of the prince and called for help.

The little mermaid left the bay, sad to think that even if her prince survived, he would never know that it was she who had saved him.

Back in her father's kingdom, her family asked what she had seen.

14

She only told them about the storm and the shipwreck, no more than that. But she often swam back to the bay, hoping in vain to see her prince. She came home every time with a heaviness in her heart that would not shift.

The other mermaids whispered among themselves and grew anxious as they watched their little sister spend too much time in her garden, holding on to her statue and crying bitter tears.

'We must talk to her,' the

oldest mermaid urged. 'Something terrible must have happened on her journeys.'

The sisters agreed, and asked their grandmother to help. At first the little mermaid refused to be comforted and would not say what made her so sad, but at last she could not resist their gentle questioning and, weeping, she poured out her story.

The little mermaid showed her sisters the royal ensign on her statue's shield and one of them said

she knew where the prince's palace
was. She told the little mermaid that
she had seen him on the beach just
the day before.

'My prince is alive!' the little
mermaid cried. Her sisters sang for
joy to see their sister happy once
more.

Now that the little mermaid knew
the prince was alive and well, she
went often to the waters outside his
palace. She grew to love his voice
as much as she adored his handsome

17

features, and she wished that she could meet him once more, face to face, and hold him in her arms as she had on that dreadful stormy day. The more she thought of this, the more she longed to be human.

'If only I had legs instead of this cumbersome tail,' she would think, as she watched the prince and saw how he moved about so gracefully. 'I could walk up and tell him that I was the one who saved him.'

Once the little mermaid had started this line of dreaming, she could think of nothing else. She decided to ask her grandmother for advice.

'Grandmother, do men live forever?' she asked one day.

Her grandmother smiled sadly and shook her head. 'No, my dear. Men die just as we do, but their life is short – not a mermaid's three hundred years. When they die, their souls leave their bodies to live in a wonderful place, far away. We turn only to foam, as your dear mother did, and stay here in the waters.'

19

'How I wish I was human,' said the little mermaid. 'I would be glad to give up my three hundred years if only I could have a soul and walk on the land instead.'

'That will never happen, little one,' said her grandmother. 'To gain a soul, a human must fall in love with you. And even if he did, you could not walk on the land on your beautiful tail.'

'My tail is not beautiful!' cried the little mermaid. 'I wish I had never been born a mermaid. I wish I had legs and walked among men!'

Her grandmother shook her head again, but said nothing as she put her arms around her granddaughter and held her as she sobbed.

If grandmother will not help me, I must go and see the sea witch, the little mermaid told herself firmly. But her heart trembled at the thought of that evil creature.

The sea witch lived alone on the other side of a fierce and angry

21

whirlpool. Many had fought their way through the furious waters to ask the sea witch for help, and few had returned. But the little mermaid did not care. Her heart was so cracked with pain, she knew that she would die anyway if she could not meet her prince again.

She waited until her sisters were busy searching for treasures and her grandmother was sleeping, and then she slipped silently from the safety of the palace.

She swam for days and days

22

without rest until she found
the whirlpool, raging and
churning on the edge of her father's
kingdom. Screwing her eyes tight,
she plunged into the howling
darkness and felt herself lashed about
by the stinging water. At last she
was spat out into a dark, slimy bog,
teeming with slithering, tentacled
creatures. They stretched out their
coiling limbs and tried to grab the
little mermaid, but her determination
propelled her through the slime and
out of their grasp. Ahead of her, she

saw the sea witch's hideous house. It was made of the skeletons of the poor creatures who had not survived their journey through the bog.

'So you have come at last,' said a creaky, sneaky voice.

The little mermaid whipped round and saw the witch lurking behind a rock. 'I . . . How did you know I was coming?' she faltered.

'I know everything,' said the witch. 'I know that your mother died when you were born, I know that your father and grandmother cherish you more than all of your sisters and I know that you fell in love with a statue and that your heart is breaking.' She cackled coldly.

The little mermaid felt the water around her turn icy. 'Not a statue,' she said, her voice bold in spite of the fear that gripped her, 'a prince. And I want you to help me meet him – I want you to give me legs.'

'Legs?' screeched the witch 'Why would you want legs when you have such a beautiful tail? You fool!

25

But who am I to tell you what you should want? You may have legs if that is your wish – at a price . . .'

The little mermaid nodded.

'Love makes fools of everyone,' the witch muttered darkly. 'Very well. Drink this potion once you reach the land. You will get your precious legs, but every step you take will be painful.'

'I don't care,' said the little mermaid.

'And you must give me your voice,' the witch added spitefully.

26

'But how will I talk to the prince? How will I tell him that I saved him and—'

'What is that to me?' the witch cut in irritably. 'I have told you my price. It is up to you.'

The little mermaid sighed and nodded sadly. 'I will take the potion and lose my tail and my voice,' she said.

The witch laughed cruelly, and a spear of lightning pierced the water. The little mermaid felt herself forced backwards by a mighty explosion

and she shut her eyes tight against
it.

When she opened them again, she
was in her garden, clutching a phial
of crystal-clear liquid.

The potion! she thought, joy
rising in her heart. I must go at
once.

When she arrived at the foot of
the cliff where the castle was, night
had fallen. The little mermaid sat
on a rock in the starlight, tilted her
pretty face up to the moon and,
lifting the phial to her lips, she

28

drained every drop of the witch's magic potion.

The liquid burned her throat as it slipped down, and the mermaid gasped in pain as, in a blinding flash of light, her silvery tail split into two slim legs. She struggled to her feet and tiptoed up the cliff path to the palace, wincing in agony at every step, as though she was walking on broken glass. A servant saw her and rushed to help, thinking that she was a poor shipwrecked girl.

Wrapping a blanket around her, he led her into the palace.

The palace servants were appalled to discover that this girl with hair as golden as the sun's rays and eyes as bright as sapphires could not speak a single word. And although the little mermaid was thrilled to be inside the walls of her beloved prince's home at last, she was sad that she could not tell everyone who she was: the mermaid who had saved the prince from drowning.

The prince was called to meet the

beautiful stranger, as it was thought
she might be a princess from a
neighbouring kingdom. Indeed, the
prince seemed to recognize her
at first, but
when she
could not
answer
him he
shook his head
sorrowfully
and said only, 'You look so like
a girl who saved me once from
drowning. But she had a voice like

31

a nightingale . . . I wish I could find that girl. I shall never forget her. She is the only person I could love.' He looked again at the little mermaid and smiled sadly. 'Please – stay with me a while.'

The mermaid nodded and smiled back at her prince. Perhaps in time she could convince him that she was the girl of whom he spoke.

The little mermaid stayed for many months with the prince. She was always at his side and he was happy for her to be there. He loved

to look on her beautiful face and
to talk to her about his hopes and
dreams. But he did not ask her to
marry him.

Every night when the prince and
his palace were sleeping, the little
mermaid would creep on to her
balcony and look out across the bay
and think of her family and the life
she had left behind.

One day the prince told the little
mermaid that he had to go on a
long journey.

'My parents wish me to marry,'

he explained. 'They have found me a girl, but I am sure she will not be as beautiful as you . . .'

The little mermaid wept and tried in vain to convince the prince with gestures that she was the girl who had saved him and that it was she whom he should marry. But the prince only thought she was sad that he was leaving and told her to be brave.

The prince was away for what seemed like a year to the little mermaid. She did not know how

34

she survived those long and lonely
days, but eventually one evening the
prince returned in a splendid golden
carriage just as the sun was setting.
The little mermaid ran out, ignoring
the pain in her feet as she rushed
to greet him. But as the carriage
approached, the little mermaid saw
that the prince had a lady with him.
A beautiful lady with long golden
hair and piercing blue eyes.

'My friend!' the prince called
when he saw the little mermaid.
'This is the girl who saved my life! I

35

have found her at last and made her
my wife.'

The little mermaid felt a pain in
her heart, sharper even than the
agony in her feet. She stood still and
watched the carriage enter the castle
gates as the palace servants cheered
and threw roses at their prince and
his bride.

The little mermaid walked down
to the bay where she had used to
swim. She looked out to sea and
felt that her heart had broken and
that she could not live without her

36

prince. She threw herself into the water, knowing that she would drown.

But as she sank into the icy depths, she heard sweet music and looked up to see strange lights. Then she felt herself being lifted up and out of the water into the sky with the lights floating around her.

'Where am I going?' she cried, her voice mysteriously restored.

'To live among the daughters of the air,' she heard. 'We are like you – we have no soul, but we can

37

earn one by good deeds. Come with us and help the needy. Blow fresh breezes to cool the sufferings of those on earth. If you help us, you may gain a soul.'

When the prince awoke the next day, he was devastated with grief to find his mysterious silent friend gone. He searched for her all over his kingdom but never found her. He did not know that she was smiling down on him from her cloud in the sky

Grandma's Warning

Philip Ardagh

On Friday morn when we set sail,

And our ship not far from the land;

We there did espy a fair, pretty maid,

With a comb and a glass in her hand.

TRADITIONAL SEA SONG

Sure you can go down to Kelpie's
Cove to make sandcastles, collect
seashells and see what you can find
in the rock pools. You can even
have a paddle or a bit of a swim, so
long as one of the bigger children is
with you. But, if one should appear,
you must never – never ever, ever,
ever – get on the back of a pretty
white pony that sometimes seems to
come out of nowhere and frolic in
the white foam along the shore.

There's no denying that such
ponies are beautiful, with their

40

flowing manes braided with silver bells and cockle shells, and their whinnying is as sweet as any music. Sure they look at you with a more intelligent eye than any horse you've met before and will ever meet again, and seem to be willing you to jump on their backs and join the fun.

But BEWARE.

These are no ordinary ponies and I know *that* as sure as I know that it's yeast that makes bread rise like the sun in the morning.

How do I know? Because of what happened to young Mary O'Connor and her little brother Michael, that's how. I remember it as plain as day because I was there and I was the lucky one.

It was on a day as beautiful as this one: sunnier, even. It was the school holidays and me and Mary and Michael had gone down to the cove bright and early. Michael found himself a starfish and put it in the little yellow tin bucket we were sharing between the three of us.

We'd found starfish before, but none as big as this fine specimen, and Michael was rightly proud.

I was using the tip of my shrimping net's wooden handle to draw pictures in the sand. I loved drawing even then and, for want of a stub of a pencil or a scrap of

43

paper, I would
draw with my
finger in the mist
on the window or
with a fork in the fluffy potato on
my plate.

That day, I was drawing a
beautiful mermaid with a comb in
one hand and a looking-glass in the
other, just like in the song. I added
seaweed for
hair, mother-
of-pearl
oyster shells

44

for the mirror and the prettiest little stones and shells I could find for a necklace. My creation looked a treat.

Just as I'd finished and stepped back to admire my handiwork, I remember hearing the lightest of laughter — like the tinkling of a bell — and a tiny splash behind me, just out to sea. I thought nothing of it at the time.

It was Mary who first saw the pony. I heard her gasp and looked up, expecting her to have found a

45

crab or an anemone or a shrimp
of a remarkable size. What I saw,
however, was a creature of such
beauty that I don't think even a
unicorn could have looked more
enchanting.

And enchanting was just the right
word, because that's what that
pony was doing. She was trying to
enchant us. To *bewitch* us.

While a unicorn, with its golden
horn of barley-sugar twist, runs like
drifting snow, this pony danced like
sunlight sparkling on the water.

46

Her mane rippled
like the finest
feathery fronds
of seaweed in
the clear waters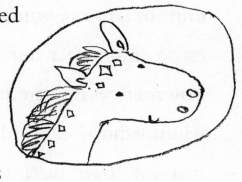
of the rock pool. Her eyes looked
into my very soul. Her expression
offered love and friendship and
unimaginable *fun*.

She reared up on her back legs
and pawed the air with her front
hooves. I saw her dainty silver
horseshoes catch the morning
sunlight and glint like diamonds. In

that moment, I wanted to climb up on to that sweet animal more than I wanted to do anything else in the whole world.

It was obvious that Mary felt the same. She was already running along the smooth wet sand towards the pony, a grin on her face as wide as an orange peel.

With just one eager leap, she was up on the animal's back and the pony trotted in a perfect circle leaving clear little horseshoe prints in the mirrored sand. Then she

stood stock still and looked at me
with such intelligence as if to say,
'You too can ride me, Kathleen, just
climb on up!'

And up I went, putting my
arms around Mary's waist while
she, in turn, held on to the pony's
fantastical mane. I saw her fingers
clutching those braided silk-like hairs
and felt a pang of jealousy. I wished
that those were *my* fingers entwined
amidst the silver bells and cockle
shells.

I felt a THUD and, moments

49

later, Michael slipping his arms around my waist in turn. If only I'd stopped then to wonder how such a small pony could accommodate all three of us upon her back. If only I'd realized that had there been ten more children — twenty, even — she would have been able to carry each and every one of us at once.

For I know now that such ponies are magical beasts. And their variety of magic is *fairy* magic, which is all well and good if you're a fairy, but it can be the most dangerous kind

50

to us mere mortals. For fairy magic
weaves its way into our souls like
no other, because the little people
are so like us in so many ways, yet
so different in others.

Before the three of us knew what
was happening, the creature dived
deep into the water, taking us into
the salty depths.

Such magical ponies can breath
underwater as easily as they can
in the fresh air but, as our captor
swam deeper and deeper, Mary,
Michael and I were in serious

51

trouble. We were sure to drown.
(We were fixed to her back as if
by the strongest glue. There was no
way that we could free ourselves
and swim to safety.)

Somehow, both Mary and I had
managed to hold our breath, but
Michael had already taken in great
gulps of seawater and, in his panic,
was probably about to breathe some
into his lungs.

The mermaid put a stop to that.

Had we not been rescued so
swiftly, not only would I not be

52

here today, but neither would any
of you children . . . because I would
never have grown up, married
your grandda, and your mother
would never have been born. So I
personally have much to thank that
mermaid for. Despite everything.

She swam up from behind a
rock and, with little more effort
than a slight wave of an elegant
hand, somehow created a separate
bubble of air around the three of
us, enabling each of us to breathe.
Looking through my bubble, the sea

53

suddenly became clear to me and I could see an underwater landscape of awesome beauty.

Michael coughed and spluttered but seemed none the worse for wear.

'Be gone,' said the mermaid to the kelpie — for that's what this pony was, a kelpie, and it is what gives the cove its name to this day.

The mermaid's voice was somehow gentle yet commanding, her hair flowing out behind her, as though blowing in a breeze. Tiny golden fishes swam amongst the jet-black locks. Her tail was made up of scales of the most gorgeous emerald green. I'd only ever seen such a colour once before and that was one Christmas on the dress of the lady up at the big house. It shimmered. And I'd thought my sand-drawn mermaid beautiful.

The fairy pony looked at the mermaid with a mixture of respect and fear, and released us from our invisible bonds.

Now, with the kelpie no longer beneath us, we floated down to

55

the seabed where the mermaid was waiting.

'Thank you!' I cried. I found it easy to talk from within the safety of the bubble.

'You saved our lives,' spluttered Michael, watching the pony gallop away through the water.

'How can we ever repay you?' said Mary.

'My name is Mavoureen,' said the mermaid. 'As to how you can repay me, child, I will find a way.' She swam around each of us three times,

56

in turn. When she had finished, she nodded as though she had made an important decision, which, we soon discovered, she most certainly had.

The little gold fishes came together at the top of her head and formed the shape of a crown. Mavoureen raised her jewel-encrusted looking-glass as though it were a sceptre. 'I have decided,' she said.

Turning to Michael, she said, 'Seeing what you have seen and knowing what you now know,

57

Michael, I cannot send you back to your people.' None of us had told her our names but there was strong magic at play. 'I give you two choices: to become a mer-person such as me, though you may well miss your soil-bound family every day for a thousand years, or to become a rock, which is a part of the earth from which you came.'

Michael spoke and, until my dying day, I swear that he was only weighing up the evidence out loud, or blurting out the options in surprise. But the moment he said, 'A rock?' that is what he became. You can still see the top of it – of the O'Connor boy's new form – when the tide is at its lowest. No limpet has ever stuck there, no seaweed grown. It remains as bare as skin.

His sister Mary was horrified. 'I offer you the same, Mary, my child,' Mavoureen said to her.

'I cannot go home? I'll never see my ma and da again?'

'You would be drowned had I not saved you,' said the mermaid. 'And now I'm offering you the chance to be my companion in this enchanted kingdom.'

'I would rather be a mermaid than a rock,' my friend Mary said, and no sooner had she spoken than the protective bubble around her disappeared and she grew a silvery tail – scale by scale – before my very eyes. In all that time, her own gaze did not leave the rock that had once been her brother, Michael.

Finally, Mavoureen the mermaid queen turned to me. 'You think me cruel, Kathleen,' she said. 'The customs of our people are different, that is all. We give and take in different ways. I ask nothing of you. You already knew of me, and captured my beauty upon the sand above.'

'You . . . you saw my picture?' I gasped, suddenly recalling the tinkle of laughter and the splash.

61

'Why yes. Your head is already filled with the wonders of my world. If you were to tell anyone of today's adventures, they'd put it down to your childish fantasies.'

And she was right, of course. When I found myself ashore, face down in the sand on the lapping water's edge, I hurried to tell others what had happened. It was put down to a tragic double-drowning and a young girl's overactive imagination. In my middle years, it was described as my artistic streak.

Now I'm old, it's put down to an old woman's fancy. But it happened, as sure as hens fear foxes.

The boy-shaped rock that came from nowhere is still there for all to see. And twice I've seen Mary as a mermaid in these past sixty years. Both times she was by her brother's rock. She was still as young and pretty as when she first grew that silvery tail. She hadn't aged a day and, I am pleased to say, she looked happy.

So yes, you can go down to

Kelpie's Cove. But stay away from any ponies. They spell nothing but TROUBLE, my young ones. And I should know.

King Miser and the Golden Touch

Anna Wilson

King Miser thrashed his majestic tail
in fury.

'One hundred gold coins? *One
hundred* gold coins! Who does he
think I am – Poseidon? Oh yes,
it would be all right if I was
as rich as a god.

Then one hundred coins would mean nothing to me.'

The king was in a mighty rage (which was quite usual, as he was rarely out of one), but this time it was serious. His only daughter, the beautiful mer-princess, Cleo, had fallen in love. Now, in itself, this was not a problem. King Miser was not a completely crusty crustacean: he had once been young and in love himself, and he did not want to deliberately upset his beloved daughter. And, although he would never admit it in public, he quite liked his daughter's fiancé, the handsome Prince Anchovy from across the bay.

But he *didn't* like the mer-prince's father, King Prawn. He was far more powerful than King Miser, and was frankly a bit of a show-off. Indeed, King Prawn liked nothing more than to lord it over his neighbour: he would ride by King Miser's cave in his chariot, pulled by a thousand silver sea horses, throwing pearls to all his adoring fans and signing autographs in glittering squid ink for the swooning mermaids who lined his path.

And he was rich. Much richer even than King Miser. Over the years, this had made King Miser jealous and bitter, so that the grumpy sea-king had started to hoard his wealth. Nowadays the only pleasure he derived from his gold was to sit and count it and gloat over it. The idea of giving any away was too much for King Miser to bear, so when King Prawn had announced that he would be very happy for his son to marry Princess Cleo, but that she would need a dowry of one hundred gold coins, he had been given a very stormy reception indeed:

'What in the wide ocean does that old Prawn-cracker want with a DOWRY, I should like to know?' shouted King Miser, causing his jellyfish servants to quiver violently. 'Isn't it enough that his precious son is marrying my beautiful daughter – and that I'm paying for the party?

69

What does old greedy-gills need a hundred gold coins for as well? Can't you find someone else to marry, Cleo? There are plenty more fish in the sea.'

Princess Cleo took a deep breath and tried to stay calm. She was used to her father's temper tantrums, but she normally managed to find a way to wrap herself around his little fin.

'Daddy darling,' she began, putting on her most pleading and adoring tone, 'you know that King

Prawn is just a bit old-fashioned. I'm sure Mummy had to come to you with a dowry before you got married . . .'

'That was different!' yelled the king, not taken in by his daughter's tail-swishing and eyelash-fluttering. (And not taking kindly to the mention of his lovely wife, who had sadly been captured by a band of pirates a few years back and had never returned. But that's another story.) 'And, in any case, it wasn't as much as one hundred gold coins!'

Cleo sighed. 'Be like that, then!' she muttered, tossing her golden hair. 'I'll have  to find the gold some other way. Prince Anchovy and I are in love and we're going to be married – there's nothing you can do about it!' She was furious. She knew that her father was a cheapskate, but this really was the last straw.

'What am I going to do? Oh, *what* am I going to do?' she cried as she swam, fast and far away from her father's palace. She did not know where she was heading or to whom she should turn for help. She knew she couldn't face Prince Anchovy in this state. Crying always made her face go red and blotchy, and she didn't want her beloved to see her like that. He might decide he didn't want to marry her after all.

Still, that would solve the problem of having to find one hundred gold coins, wouldn't it? Princess Cleo thought miserably.

73

She came to a bay and swam up
near the surface, where there were
countless sparkling rock pools. It
seemed like a good place to take a
rest and try to think things through,
so Cleo flopped down on to a rock
and, basking in the sunlight filtering
through the shallow water, she took
out her mother-of-pearl hairbrush.
Brushing her hair always made
her feel better. She soon got into a
soothing rhythm, pulling out a few
stray shrimps and starfish as she
sang to herself.

'Ah!' said a rasping voice. 'There is nothing lovelier than a mermaid's song!'

Cleo felt a chill run down the length of her tail. 'Who's that?' she called.

'Down here!' said the voice.

Cleo peered down into the dark depths of the bay and made out a small hunched shape, swimming back and forth beneath her. She felt her scales stand on end as it occurred to her that she did not know where she was, and that sea monsters might be lurking, waiting to pounce at any moment.

'Don't be afraid – I won't bite!' came the voice. 'I'm here to help you, my pretty. A little fish told me your love life is on the rocks – am I right?'

'Who are you?' Cleo called down to the dark figure. 'And how do you know about me?'

'Everyone knows about you, dearie,' said the voice. 'The sea-waves have been a-quiver with news about the royal wedding for weeks, you know. We've all been very excited about it. But now it seems the wedding's off unless you can persuade your father to come up with the cash for your in-laws-to-be – am I right? Come closer so that we can have a proper chat, my pretty.'

Cleo had never been one for deep-sea diving. It made her short of breath – and anyway, she was afraid of the dark. She always had a glow-in-the-dark jellyfish by her seabed at night. But this creature, whoever it was, seemed to understand her problems, and was offering to help her . . . She decided to take the plunge.

As Cleo's eyes grew accustomed to the murky water, she saw that the creature was a mermaid – but not a pretty one. For a start, her hair was black with streaks of grey, not the blonde of other mermaids. And her face was etched with deep wrinkles, as was her tail, which was as black and dull grey as her hair. She had long, bony fingers with nails like claws, and she didn't appear to have any teeth. (No wonder she'd said she wouldn't bite.)

She was a sea witch.

Her name was Costia and she had lived in the deep, dark waters on the edge of King Miser's kingdom since Cleo was a mer-baby. She knew everyone and everything, and had magical powers most mermaids had only heard about in stories. She had never liked King Miser. He had cast her out after she'd refused to grant him a wish many years ago – a wish to become richer than King Prawn.

'H-h-h-hello,' stammered Cleo. She had never heard of Costia before, but she was still frightened by the ugly old crone.

'Hello to you, my dearie,' said Costia. 'Come closer, can't you?'

Cleo felt another chill shiver down her tail, but did as she was asked.

'So,' the sea witch continued, 'you need gold.'

'Ye-yes,' replied Cleo.

'Well, you've come to the right place,' said Costia.

Cleo looked around her, as if hoping to find a pile of gold coins hiding in the dark.

Costia sniggered nastily. 'Oh, *I* don't have any, I'm afraid. What would I do with gold down here, anyway?'

She hesitated, enjoying the look of disappointment on the poor mermaid's face. 'But I *can* make sure your daddy has more gold

81

than even *he* can handle, if you'll agree to a couple of rules,' she said finally.

'Oh yes! Anything!' Cleo cried. 'Anything if it means I can marry dear Anchovy! I'm desperate!'

'You must be if you want to marry a merman with a name like that,' Costia muttered, and then said aloud: 'What about giving Daddy a magical gift, eh? Let me think . . . how about the power to change any object into gold? I think even King Miser would be willing to part with

82

a few measly gold coins if he had that power, don't you?'

Cleo gulped and nodded nervously. It certainly sounded like an amazing gift.

'No sooner said than done!' cried Costia, cackling loudly. 'Your father is this very minute turning all the objects he possesses into gold. By the time you get home, he will have more gold than he knows what to do with. But listen,' she said, pointing a knobbly finger at the mermaid. 'These are the rules:

you *must* tell your father that this power is a gift from Costia, the wise woman of the sea. In return for this gift, he must let me come back to live in the heart of his kingdom where I belong. You must also tell him that he will only keep the gift if he gives you the one hundred gold coins *immediately* on your return. And remember, child,' the wizened old sea witch went on, fixing Cleo with a glare of granite, 'EVERYTHING he touches will turn to gold.

84

EVERYTHING. Be sure to tell him that.'

Cleo was so overjoyed that she would at last be marrying her prince that she didn't really pay much attention to the boring bits. She just said, 'Yes, yes, whatever! Oh, thank you!' and rushed to hug the old mermaid. It was a bit of a slimy cuddle, but the princess was too happy to notice.

'I'm going home right away to tell Daddy and darling Anchovy the good news!' she cried.

85

Costia narrowed her black eyes
and sneered as the mer-princess
swished her way out of the dark and
gloomy cave. 'A gift that's worth its
weight in gold,' she muttered. 'Let's
see what that old oyster does with it.'

Back at King Miser's palace the
old king was in a party mood,
cheering and singing sea songs,
surrounded by ever-growing piles
of golden objects. He was sitting on
his throne, which was now made of
gold, rather than the grey rock it

had once been, and was ordering his jellyfish servants to bring more and more objects for him to touch. They brought cups and plates and statues and vases and shells and pebbles and tiny fishes and seaweed – even handfuls of sand from the seabed were turned to gold.

'Marvellous, marvellous miracle!' the king was shouting. 'At last I am richer than King Prawn! That stupid old sea witch had said it would end in disaster if I ever became too rich! What does she know?' he crowed.

87

'I wish he'd clam up,' one of his servants muttered moodily.

'Yes,' agreed another. 'I think I preferred him when he was grumpy.'

Cleo arrived back in time to see her father touch a vase of sea anemones and turn them into dazzling gold. Cleo was so excited, she rushed to embrace her father, shouting as she did so, 'Father! It worked! The magic has worked! Now can I have the money to marry Prince Anch—?'

But she couldn't finish, because

88

the moment her father's arms encircled her she turned to gold.

King Miser was horrified. For the first time in his life, he was speechless.

For about thirty seconds.

And then he roared. He roared and roared with such terrifying force that his jellyfish servants melted clean away. The sea around the kingdom turned blacker than squid ink and a storm rocked the water right down to the seabed. All that was left of the palace was the golden objects, the golden mer-princess and King Miser – alone on his golden throne.

The storm died down eventually, and King Miser sat staring at his shining statue of a daughter, his heart heavy with misery and regret.

Maybe the storm has washed away the evil magic, the king thought to himself, and got up from his throne to fetch himself a goblet of wine to calm his nerves. He found a flask that had wedged itself between a golden vase and a golden cabinet during the storm, but as soon as the king touched the flask of wine, the container and the liquid inside it turned to gold.

91

Days and weeks passed, and still the magic did not wear off. Cleo remained a golden statue, and any little crumb of food or drop of drink that the king could find also turned to gold the second he touched it. King Miser became weak and miserable and took to sitting on his golden throne, staring at his daughter and weeping.

No one in the kingdom dared to come to the palace. They were all terrified of being turned into gold themselves. The whole kingdom had become a dark and miserable place to live. The mer-people missed their princess and everyone was fed up because there couldn't be a royal wedding any more.

No one was more fed up than the handsome Prince Anchovy. 'What has happened to Cleo?' he shouted, swimming furiously up and down in front of his father's throne. 'I have called, I have written, I have sent presents, but she's not responding. She's not speaking to me! This is all your fault, Dad,' he said, turning

on his father. 'If you hadn't insisted
on this rotten dowry of one hundred
coins, we'd be married by now! I'm
going over there right away and
I'm going to marry her on the spot,
dowry or no dowry. Just try and
stop me!'

King Prawn had been trying to
have his afternoon snooze and was
not amused by his son's constant
charging up and down.

'Oh for Poseidon's sake, do
whatever you like!' he said irritably.
'Take the chariot, marry the

mermaid and be done with it. Just don't come swimming to me if it doesn't work out.'

Prince Anchovy did not give his father time to change his mind. He dashed to his room and dragged a comb through his flowing golden locks, put on his most dashing outfit, grabbed the wedding ring he'd been keeping for Cleo and swished out of the palace to the stable yard. The chariot was there with the thousand silver sea horses already harnessed. He swam to his seat and gave the

order: 'Full speed to King
Miser's palace!'

When the mer-
people of King Miser's
kingdom saw the chariot coming
they hid behind their rocks in terror
and whispered to one another.

'We've got to tell him,' said one
mermaid. 'If he goes in there, he'll
be turned into a statue too.'

But no one was brave enough
to talk to the prince, so they just
hovered and watched him go to the
palace door and knock.

Of course there was no answer.

'Well, I must say this is a bit fishy,' he said out loud. 'Where is everybody? Where is Cleo? Maybe she doesn't love me any more. Maybe she's left to marry someone else.'

And he gulped back tears.

'Don't be such a wet fish,' came a rasping voice from the palace steps.

'Urgh!' said Prince Anchovy, leaping back in horror at the sight of the wizened old hag.

'Charming!' said Costia. 'You

97

should be careful how you talk to me, young man. I'm a sea witch, and I'm probably your last hope if you ever want to see your darling fiancée again,' she added menacingly.

The mer-prince looked the barnacled old bag up and down. What was she talking about? Had she captured poor Cleo? *Better play along*, he thought to himself. Anything was worth a try if it meant he would see Cleo again.

98

'Erm, OK. Thank you, er, madam,' he said. (Nothing in his palace upbringing had quite prepared him for how to address a sea witch.)

Costia growled. 'Follow me,' she said, and slithered round the back of the palace.

The sea witch led Prince Anchovy into the throne room and, flinging out her bony arm, she said sarcastically, 'There, Your Royal Saltiness. *There's* your darling princess!'

99

It was a good job that Prince Anchovy was a cold-blooded creature, otherwise his blood would have frozen at the sight. There before him was the once proud and mighty King Miser, now reduced to a shrivelled dried-out whimpering old merman. And in front of the throne was what appeared to be a beautiful golden statue—

'Cleo!' Prince Anchovy cried, and rushed over to her. 'Cleo, what's happened to you? Oh my darling!'

'I'll tell you what's happened to her,' said Costia. 'That nasty old merman over there, the one who was going to be your father-in-law, he turned his own daughter into gold, didn't he?'

'W-w-w-what?' cried Prince Anchovy, and he rushed to the throne, so mad with anger he thought he might punch the old sea-king squarely on the nose.

'STOP!' cried King Miser, suddenly springing to life. 'Don't come near me! I'm doomed! If you

101

touch me, you'll turn to gold too!
I'm sick of the sight of the stuff. I
never want to see any more gold
again for as long as I live.'

Costia cackled. 'Is that right,
Your Majesty?'

King Miser squinted at the sea
witch. 'Costia? What are you doing
here? I thought I'd banished you
years ago!'

'Hmmm, yes, you did,' the sea
witch said, nodding. 'I think the
conversation went something like
this, "Costia, I want wealth beyond

102

my wildest dreams." "Your Majesty, I don't think that would be a very good idea." "Go and rot in the deepest darkest ocean then, you old hag!"'

'Yes, yes,' said the old king wearily. 'Well, I'm sorry. You win. It turns out you were right all along. Having wealth beyond my wildest dreams has left me old, sad and lonely. Can you help me, Costia? You can come back to the kingdom. You can even live in the palace, if you like. It would nice

to have the company,' he added
lamely.

Costia stared at the desperate sea-
king in amazement. 'I thought an
old leopard shark like you would
never change his spots,' she said.

'Just bring Cleo back to me and
I'll do anything you want,' said the
weak old sea-king.

Costia nodded, swam over to
Cleo and touched her lightly on the
shoulder. Immediately life flooded
back into the statue; the only
 gold that was left was

the natural blonde locks of the mer-princess's hair.

So the mer-people of King Miser's kingdom got their royal wedding, Prince Anchovy got his bride and Princess Cleo her groom. And, much to everyone's surprise, King Prawn even got his one hundred gold coins.

'After all, what do I want with money?' said King Miser to Costia at the wedding reception as he watched his beautiful daughter

105

dancing and laughing with her new husband. 'Cleo's happiness is worth its weight in gold to me.'

Can You Catch a Mermaid?

Jane Ray

Have you ever seen a mermaid?

Have you ever seen a shimmering

tail and some strands of greeny-gold

hair turning in the water?

Maybe not.

But did you know that sometimes,

just sometimes, a mermaid can

turn her fishy tail to legs and come ashore? As long as she keeps hold of something from her ocean home, she can return to the water. But, if she should lose that something, she is trapped on land forever.

This is the story of Eliza, who really did see a mermaid.

Eliza lived with her father, Tom, who was a fisherman. Just him and her,

comfortable and close, taking care
of each other.

'You are my little dolphin,' he
would say, holding Eliza tight in
his arms, like the harbour walls
protecting the little boats.

Eliza was shy and liked to play
by herself, searching in rock pools
and collecting pebbles and shells.
Sometimes Tom worried about her.

'Why don't you go off and play
with the other children?' he would
say.

But Eliza would shake her head.

'I only want to be with you,' she said.

Every day, Eliza waved goodbye to her father as she set off in his fishing boat.

'What shall I bring you for tea today, little dolphin?' he would say. 'Sardines or skate? Hake or herring? Winkles, cockles or crab?'

And every day Eliza answered, 'Can you catch a mermaid?'

One evening, as Eliza was waiting for the chug-chug-chug of her

father's boat, she saw a girl of about
her own age playing at the water's
edge. They smiled at each other
shyly. The girl didn't frighten Eliza
like the children at school. Instead
Eliza felt curious and wanted to talk
to her.

The next morning, when Tom
set off in his boat, the little girl
was there again. She gave Eliza a
shell that was pink and gold, and
when Eliza put it to her ear it
sang:

Can I be your friend, Eliza? Come

and play with me,

Where the dolphins leap and the

seagulls cry,

And the sand becomes the sea.

The girls played together all day. By the time evening came, and it was time for Eliza to go home, it felt as if they had known each other all their lives. The girl's name was Freya and she had long greeny-gold hair and pale, pale skin. Her eyes were the colour of stormy seas and all about her was the scent of salt and rock pools. Around her neck she carried a beautiful little mirror, inlaid with pieces of coral and mother-of-pearl.

'Sing with me, Eliza,' Freya called, and she taught Eliza songs so beautiful that they had to be shared.

'Dance with me, Eliza,' she said, and they danced together like a sea breeze.

Eliza didn't know where Freya came from or where she went to at night. Sometimes she was there and sometimes she wasn't, and then Eliza was as lonely as a sandpiper.

But one morning, Eliza found Freya crying, running up and down at the water's edge, wringing her hands.

'I've lost my mirror. It's gone, it's gone! Oh, please help me to find it – please! For I can't go home with it. Without it I can't ever go home!' And then, Eliza realized who Freya was.

Tom had told Eliza all about the

114

mermaids, how they can come on to the land and go back into the sea, if they keep something special from their ocean home with them. Freya was a mermaid, and the little mirror was her special thing.

Eliza took Freya's hand. 'Don't worry,' she said. 'We'll find your mirror.'

Eliza and Freya searched all day, back and forth like beachcombers along the shoreline. But they couldn't find the mirror. That night, Eliza took her friend home and she and Tom cared for the little mermaid as if she was their own.

Deep in the ocean, Freya's mother was looking for her daughter and, when the waves whispered the terrible news that the mirror was lost and with it her child, her grief was great and unspeakable. Her little Freya! That night, terrible storms battered the coast where Freya was stranded.

Meanwhile, Freya stayed with Eliza and Tom, and shared their

116

food and their stories and Eliza's
little bed. But Freya was unhappy.
She fretted for her family and her
ocean home. Every morning she set
out to search for the mirror.

Now, Eliza had a secret. A few
days after Freya's arrival, they were
on the beach as usual, looking for
the lost mirror. Eliza clambered on

the rocks where the sea rushed at high tide and there she found the mirror, covered in seaweed. She washed it quickly but, instead of giving it back to Freya as she knew she should, she put it in her pocket. Eliza couldn't bear for Freya to leave.

Eliza took the mirror home and hit it in her secret box. And when she was quite alone, she took it out and looked at herself in the watery glass. *I'll give it to Freya tomorrow*, she thought.

But the days passed, and still Eliza kept the mirror secret.

The days passed and Freya grew thinner and even paler. She no longer laughed or danced on the sand, but spent her days searching, searching, searching for the lost mirror.

The other families began to mutter about Freya. Their catches had dwindled to almost nothing since she had arrived and now the weather was so dark and stormy it

119

was dangerous to put out to sea at
all.

One wild night,
Eliza couldn't sleep.
The waves crashed
against the harbour wall. Eliza
picked up the pink-and-gold shell
that Freya had given her when
they'd first met and put it to her
ear. At first Eliza heard only the
storm outside. Then, very faintly,
she heard a voice sighing, 'Let me
go, let me go home.'

Eliza looked at Freya sleeping

restlessly at her side. She knew what she must do. She crept to her hiding place, took out the mirror and gently tucked it into Freya's hand. Then she climbed back into bed and fell into a deep sleep.

In the morning the wind had dropped. Pale sunshine spilled into the room. Freya was gone.

Tom set sail on a calm sea. Before he left, he held Eliza extra tight. 'What shall I bring you today, my brave little dolphin?'

121

Eliza smiled a sad smile.

That day, Tom came back with nets full of fish. And from then on the village fishing nets were always full, and Tom's was the fullest of all.

And that day, Eliza made new friends. Now she loves playing with the other children. They collect shells and Eliza shows them how to build mermaids out of sand. When she puts the beautiful pink-and-gold shell to her ear she still hears Freya's sweet voice singing to her, and the songs she sings are of her ocean home and the silver fishes that play there.

And sometimes, in still rock pools or in the deep green ocean, when Eliza is out in Tom's boat, she thinks she sees Freya smiling up at her through the water.

Or maybe it's her own reflection.

Marina Makes a Splash

Vic Parker

'Ouch! . . . Eeek! . . . OWWW!'
the little mermaid moaned as her
mother struggled to comb out her
wild and
wiry shock
of seaweed-
green hair.

'Oh, Marina,' her mother sighed. 'Why couldn't you have had long, lovely hair like the rest of us? Just look at Coral and Pearl . . .' She gestured to Marina's two older sisters, who looked the picture of mermaid perfection. Coral's hair curled and twirled to her waist, a gorgeous, glossy red. Pearl's hair rippled to the tip of her tail, a sleek sheet of shining silver. Marina's mother flicked back her own lustrous locks. 'My jet-black waves have always been my crowning glory.'

She gave another big sigh. 'But you, Marina – well, I despair of your tangled tresses. Your hair is totally untameable – just like you.'

Marina rolled her eyes. *Here we go again*, she thought.

'Yes, Marina,' cut in Coral. 'And it's not only your hair that's a problem. Look at the rest of you! There's sea-salt going crusty behind your ears, there's sand under your fingernails and I can't remember the last time that you polished your tail!'

126

'It was only last new moon!'
Marina pointed out. 'But my scales
just seem to get dull and chipped
faster than everyone else's.'

'It's because of your behaviour!'
piped up Pearl. 'You're always
dashing and darting about,
exploring silly shipwrecks and boring
underwater caves, going diving with
dolphins and playing with porpoises
like some wild mer-child, instead
of acting like the well-brought-up
young lady you're supposed to be.
You really let us down with your

127

unmermaidlike behaviour. Everyone laughs at us when we go out with you!'

'I can't help it!' Marina protested. 'I've just got too much energy. I'd far rather go racing through the ocean, fast and free, than perch on the rocks, primping and preening like you pair of posers—'

'Mum!' both Coral and Pearl exploded at once. 'Did you hear what she—'

'Enough, girls!' their mother demanded, holding up her hand

128

for silence. 'Arguing won't help us decide what in the seven seas we're going to do with Marina's hair for the Deeps' Dash and Dance tomorrow.'

All the merfolk were looking forward to the annual Deeps' Dash and Dance – a dangerous sea-horse race to find the bravest, strongest, most skilful merman rider, followed by a big, posh ball to celebrate. Everyone who was anyone would be there – it was THE place to see and be seen.

129

'Just think,' breathed Pearl dreamily, 'this year the band that's playing at the ball is Bob Marlin and the Whales! I can't believe I'm going to be in the same room as the famous Bob Marlin – he's such a dishy fishy. I'd give anything to get close to him . . . to talk to him . . . maybe even to touch him . . .'

'Never mind Bob Marlin,' sneered Coral. 'The chief editor for *Fin* fashion magazine is going to be there, the glamorous Miss Anemone Spike. She'll be looking

130

for mermaids beautiful enough to
be photographed for the magazine
– and you know how I've always
longed to be a model. I might get
spotted . . .'

'Well, I'm not going!' interrupted
Marina. 'I don't care about the
stupid dance! I don't care about
stupid Bob Marlin, I don't care
about stupid fashion models and
most of all I DON'T CARE
ABOUT MY STUPID HAIR!' She
grabbed the comb from her mum,
threw it away as far as she could

131

and swam off at top speed. In just
a few flicks of her tail she had
disappeared into the blue, among
the darting shoals of rainbow-
coloured fish . . .

But Marina *did* care. She cared very
much that other merfolk laughed
because her hair was fuzzy and
frizzy like feathery plant fronds. She
cared very much that she didn't
fit in because she loved speed and
excitement and adventure, while
the other mermaids preferred acting

132

like prim and pouty princesses. With her heart aching, Marina found her favourite hiding place – an underwater rock pool far away from the usual merfolk hangouts. She sat on a gravelly mound, put her head in her hands and began to cry.

Marina wasn't left moping on her own for long. Soon, a small, raggedy-looking sea horse zipped up to her and nudged her with his nose.

'Hey, Marina, I've been looking for you all over,' he said. 'What's up?'

133

'Oh, Sandy,' Marina said with a big sob. 'You really are my only friend in all the world. Everyone else thinks I'm an embarrassment. It's the Deeps' Dash and Dance tomorrow, and I can't go because everyone will make fun of me — most of all, because of my hair.'

'Whatever's wrong with it?' Sandy remarked, flipping at a strand with his fin. 'I've always thought it's lovely.'

'That's because you're a sea horse, silly,' sniffed Marina. 'If you were one of us merfolk, you'd think it was horrid and ugly. It's crispy and crimped and the colour's all wrong.'

'Well, you know what they say: hair today, gone tomorrow — or something like that,' said Sandy wisely. 'But, if it's really upsetting

135

you, we should do something about it.' He thought for a second. 'Hey, why don't we try dyeing it? We could use squid ink to darken it to a deep emerald shade.'

'Oh, Sandy, you're so kind,' said Marina, her eyes shining with tears. 'Do you really think it will work?'

'Nothing ventured, nothing lost – or something like that,' said the small sea horse with a grin.

Sandy zigzagged off to the sandbanks where the Armstrong squid family lived. He was very

nervous when he asked for some
ink, because he knew that squid
could be unfriendly and obstinate
creatures at the best of times.

'Hmm, let me see . . .' Mrs
Armstrong considered, looking
rather grumpy. 'Well . . . the other
mermaids always swim past us with
their noses in the air, but Marina's
not snobby and stand-offish like
them. She's always got time for
a quick game of hide-and-seek
with the children. So I suppose the
answer's yes.'

137

'I love Marina,' the littlest squid piped up shyly. 'She shows me where the very best hiding places are.'

'When I hurt my tentacle,' said the second littlest, 'she wrapped it in seaweed and kissed it better.' And he blushed.

'Marina's my best friend,' said Sandy proudly, and he held out a shell quickly before Mrs Armstrong could change her mind. Each squid squirted a little of their precious ink

into it. Then Sandy thanked them
and swam ever so carefully back to
the little mermaid, determined not to
spill a drop.

Marina was delighted. Straight
away, she leaned over a nearby
rock pool and Sandy helped her
wash her hair in the glossy ink.

'What does it look like?' asked
Marina, straightening up and
patting her head anxiously.

'Erm . . . well . . . your hair's
not green any more . . . It's
different – yes, definitely

different,' stuttered Sandy, not quite looking Marina in the eye.

'But do you mean good-different or bad-different?' Marina pressed.

'Oh dear,' blustered Sandy, his face turning red. 'I can't fib to you – it's a disaster. Your hair's turned the colour of a stormcloud – a dull, dingy and dirty dark grey!'

'Oooh noo!' moaned Marina. 'It sounds worse than before. Whatever am I going to do now?'

'Don't worry, I'm sure we can fix it. You know what they say: it'll all get wet in the wash – or something like that,' Sandy said confidently. 'Now, let's think . . .' He bobbed up and down, concentrating hard. 'Perhaps we should try a hot mud-conditioning treatment to see if we can make it smooth and sleek and shiny.'

Marina brightened up slightly. 'Well, I suppose it's worth a try,' she said.

Sandy led the little mermaid to a hot undersea spring, where boiling smoky water bubbled up from deep

141

within the seabed. The scorching
vent was surrounded by luscious
mud, and the small sea horse helped
Marina to smother her hair in the
hot, squelchy muck. Then they both
sat and waited . . . and waited . . .
and waited . . .

'How long do you think before it
starts to work?' Marina wondered.

'I'm not sure,' Sandy said. 'But
it looks to me like it's pretty well
sunk in,' he remarked, looking

nervously at the gloopy
ooze all over Marina's

142

head. 'Let's rinse it off and see how beautifully shiny your hair is now.'

But the thick mud had clagged and clogged and clung, sticking to Marina's locks in great gobbets and lumps.

'Oh, this hasn't worked at all!' she wailed. 'It's not washing out . . . I bet these muddy strands look like waving tentacles! Everyone will think I'm some sort of sea monster if I turn up to the Deeps' Dash and Dance like this! What shall I do?'

'Don't panic!' instructed Sandy, trying to calm the desperate mermaid down. 'Where there's a will, there's a whale – or something like that. We'll just have to come up with another plan. Now think, Sandy . . . think, think . . .' The small sea horse zigzagged back and forth in the water, racking his brain for ideas. 'I've got it!' he announced finally. 'If we washed your hair with a powder of the finest golden sand grains and crushed silvery seashells,

144

it would surely add some sparkle and shine.'

'Do you really think so?' asked Marina hopefully.

'Of course!' beamed Sandy. 'Let's do it!' And he hurried to grind the seashells and mix in the sand, and help the little mermaid to wash her hair once again.

'So . . .' said Marina, when they were finished. 'What do you reckon?'

'Oh dear . . .' sighed Sandy,

shaking his head. 'Oh dear, oh dear, oh dear.'

'What?' asked Marina.

'Well,' Sandy explained, 'your hair's still storm-cloud grey and coated in mud, but now it's caked in sand grains and seashell dust too.'

'Oh, whatever shall I do?' Marina yelped. 'I was only trying to be like everyone else and now I'm even more different than ever. I must look ridiculous!'

Sandy took a deep breath. 'It's such a mess, there's only one thing for it,' he said firmly. 'We'll have to cut it all off—'

'Cut it off!' Marina howled. 'My mother will kill me . . .'

'But it will get rid of most of the ink dye and the mud lumps and the clumps of sand and seashell,' Sandy explained gently. 'There's just nothing else for it . . .'

Marina sat down glumly. 'I suppose you're right,' she gulped. 'Go on, then . . . grab a razor shell . . . I'm ready.'

So the small sea horse sliced and

147

slashed, sheared and shaved, and Marina's dirty, damaged hair fell all around her in hunks and chunks.

The little mermaid put her hands up to her head and felt all over with her fingertips . . . It felt short . . . it felt spiky . . . it felt sassy . . . it felt fun and free . . . Marina began to smile.

'Wheee!' she cried, turning somersaults in the water. 'My hair feels fantastic!'

Sandy couldn't believe his eyes. He breathed a huge sigh of relief. 'I'm really glad you're pleased,' he said with a grin, 'but try not to get too excited. You know that everyone's going to say you look like a boy.'

'I don't care what everyone says!' Marina sang. 'I don't care what everyone thinks! I *love* it.' And she cartwheeled for joy across the seabed, her tail stirring up arcs of bubbles in the water.

'Marina, Marina, stop!' Sandy

shouted, all of a sudden. 'I've had another idea!'

'If it's making a wig out of seaweed, you can forget it,' Marina yelled back, speeding through the waves.

'No – this is a much, much better idea,' Sandy insisted. 'Listen – now you look like a boy, why don't we enter the Deeps' Dash tomorrow? It's only for mermen – but once you're dressed as a jockey, no one could ever tell that you're actually a mermaid. I may not be one of the

150

biggest, best-looking sea horses in the ocean, but you know that I'm one certainly one of the speediest – and I don't know of any merfolk that are faster, braver and bolder than you . . . What do you say? . . . Come on, let's enter the race and show them that you're not a nobody to be sniggered and smirked at.'

Marina was silent for a moment. She chewed a fingernail thoughtfully. Then she beamed. 'I love you, Sandy,' she said.

151

'What are friends for?' he chuckled. 'Just remember: the world is your lobster – or something like that.'

The next day, when the racers and riders swam up to the starting line of the Deeps' Dash, there was a small sea horse and a little jockey that no one had ever seen before. Merfolk from far and wide had turned out to support their favourites and the enormous crowd was buzzing with excitement. However, among all the

152

cheers and cries of encouragement were some sniggers and calls of, 'Go home, tiddler!' and, 'Give up now, minnow!'

Marina tried not to listen. She was shaking so badly with nerves she was sure that somebody would spot she was an imposter. But the other jockeys were all far too busy trying to control their snorting steeds to notice Marina trembling as she held on tightly to her small sea horse's reins.

Then the starter blew his conch

153

shell – and they were off! Marina and Sandy swam so hard the race flew by in the blink of an eye . . .

The first danger to overcome was a white-water whirlpool. The strong currents were deadly and one merman and his sea horse were swirled away, never to be seen again. But Sandy and Marina were used to wild waters – after all, they had often played tag among rocks where crashing breakers smashed shells to smithereens as they plunged and foamed. 'Wheee!' cried Marina, as she and Sandy were whisked around by the whirlpool before speeding safely out the other side.

Next, they had to negotiate a quicksand quagmire. Another merman and his sea horse were

155

sucked down to a sticky end. But Marina and Sandy were much lighter and nimbler than the muscley male riders and their hefty horses. Flicking their tails as hard as they could, they floated softly over the slurping sand.

Then the riders and racers headed for an ancient, collapsing shipwreck in the midst of the shark hunting grounds. Marina and Sandy slowed their pace, their hearts pounding. They were used to ducking and diving through some of the deepest and darkest shipwrecks in all the ocean – but lean mean fish with razor-sharp teeth and big bad appetites were a completely different matter.

'You know what they say,' whispered Sandy, 'we're in a pretty kettle of sharks – or something like that.'

Bravely, the little mermaid and her sea horse zipped through the ruins, causing barely a ripple or a murmur to attract attention. Yet just as they cleared the barnacle-crusted bow of the shipwreck, a dead-eyed shark came cruising up behind them, grinning greedily.

'Swim for your life!' yelled Sandy, and – *SNAP!* – the shark found himself biting down on empty bubbles where the speedy mermaid and sea horse had been, seconds before.

Last of all, they had to brave the pitch-black, cavernous lair of a sea witch.

'Don't worry,' Marina urged Sandy, as they swam through the

158

icy-cold darkness. 'I sometimes come here to help the sea witch with her garden. She may know magic, but no one can grow seagrass like I can! I'm sure she won't try to stop us . . .' Sure enough, the sea witch took her enchanted fishing net in her gnarled old fingers and cast it wide, catching several competitors and dragging them down into her den. But not once did she throw the net anywhere near Marina and Sandy.

They made it out into clearer

waters, and with one final burst of speed they sprang forward – FIRST OVER THE FINISHING LINE!

Marina and Sandy found themselves surrounded by merfolk, clapping and cheering and congratulating them. 'I knew we could do it,' the small sea horse told the little mermaid, as she was hoisted aloft on everyone's shoulders. 'After all, if you have faith, you can move fountains – or something like that.'

★

160

Marina's mother and sisters hadn't been to watch the race – they were far too busy making themselves beautiful for the Deeps' Dance which was to follow. They quivered with excitement as they arrived, bedecked in their finest.

'Oooh look, there's Anemone Spike from *Fin* magazine,' squealed Coral. 'Doesn't she look elegant and fabulous? Do you think she's noticed me yet?' Coral tried to swim with attitude past the famous fashion guru, and ended up tripping over

161

her own tail and falling flat on her face.

'Can it, Coral!' hissed Pearl. 'Here comes Bob Marlin and the Whalers – isn't he just the coolest guy in all the ocean? They're about to play!' She dashed to the front of the ballroom to dance where the singer would be most likely to see her – but hundreds of other mermaids had the same idea, and Pearl was flattened and trampled in the rush.

In the end, the two humiliated sisters watched the band from the

162

back of the ballroom, red-faced and fed up, their enjoyment completely spoiled. They sulked and sulked till the end of the evening when an announcement was made: 'And, finally, mermaids and mermen, we would like to present the trophy for the Deeps' Dash. Three cheers for this year's winners: Hip hip hooray! Hip hip hooray! Hip hip hooray!'

Marina's mother, Coral and Pearl watched open-mouthed

as Marina and her small sea-horse friend made their way up on to the stage. 'But . . . but . . .' Marina's mother blustered. 'I don't believe it! . . . That's our Marina . . . I hardly recognize her – whatever has she done to her hair?'

As Marina and Sandy were handed a huge silver trophy and everyone roared with applause, Pearl and Coral looked at each other, green with jealousy.

'Are you thinking what I'm thinking?' Coral spat.

164

'Yes – let's go,' hissed Pearl.

And the sisters pushed their way forward to the front of the crowd.

'We have an announcement of our own,' Coral shouted at the top of her voice, so everyone could hear.

'That so-called merman isn't a merman at all,' yelled Pearl. 'She's actually a mermaid. So you can't give them the trophy.'

'In fact, they should be disqualified!' finished Coral.

Everyone fell into a stunned

165

silence and stared questioningly at the little jockey.

'It's true,' Marina murmured. 'I'm not a champion rider after all. I'm just a misfit mermaid with dodgy hair.'

'I wouldn't call that hair dodgy at all, dahling,' cut in Anemone Spike, striding towards Marina and running her fingers through the elfin haircut. 'I'd call it style, I'd call it pizzazz, I'd call it *fashion*. In fact, if you come and see me next week, I'd like to feature you in my magazine.'

'Yeah, you're the only hip and happening chick in a room full of boring babes, honey,' growled Bob Marlin. 'I'll get my people to call your people and maybe we can hook up.'

All at once there were claps and cheers and whoops of delight, then calls of congratulations once more. Marina and Sandy beamed from ear to ear, and raised their winner's trophy up high for all to see.

And that is how every young mermaid who wanted to be fashionable that year came to cut their long hair into a short sea-urchin crop – including Marina's two sisters, Coral and Pearl.

Of course, Marina couldn't think of anything worse than posing for a fashion photo shoot or going on a date with Bob Marlin. 'Why don't you go along to see Anemone

Spike in my place?' Marina kindly told Coral. 'And why don't you meet Bob Marlin instead of me?' she generously suggested to Pearl. And that is how Coral came to appear on the cover of *Fin* fashion magazine, and how Pearl came to marry a rock star.

And what happened to Marina? Well, the merfolk changed the sea-horse racing rules in her honour, so mermaids could compete alongside mermen. She and Sandy entered race after race – winning them all –

and became the greatest sea-horse-and-rider partnership ever to speed through the oceans. Which may not surprise you, because, of course, you know what they say: fortune favours the fastest – or something like that.

It's Raining (Mer)men!

Ian Billings

Captain Copperknuckle, the
grimmest and dimmest pirate ever
to sail the seven seas, was in a very
bad mood.

'I'm in a very bad mood!'
he announced to his cowering
crew through a large wooden

megaphone. He took a hearty chomp from his apple and continued, spitting pips with each breath, 'We have been at sea for nine months and each day we've failed in our mission to find a mermaid!'

The crew of the good ship *Weevil* exchanged nervous glances. They were a hardy bunch of pirates, but they were very scared of their boss. He had forced

them to sail the seas searching
for a mermaid to take home to
Blighty. Zoos paid handsome prices
for unseen creatures of the deep,
and a mermaid would fetch the
handsomest price of all.

'We are within three days' sail of
Portsmouth and I want a mermaid
in my bathtub before we drop
anchor!' He banged his fist on the
ship's wheel and it whizzed round.

The crew groaned under their
breaths. Captain Copperknuckle
was a fearsome fellow – whenever

173

he was unhappy (which was a lot of the time) he would simply fire a crew member. He even kept a special cannon, Belching Bessy, for this very purpose.

'Is someone a-groaning?' snarled the captain, scanning his beady eye across the crew.

'Noooooooooooooooooooooo!' they all muttered back.

Captain Copperknuckle strode down the bridge. He was a short man with a long black beard that swished as he walked.

174

'Just remember – if you don't
get me my mermaid – you'll all be
fired!'

That night, as the night watchman
slept in the crow's nest and the stars
twinkled their hardest to cheer up
the pirates, there were mutterings,
mumblings and moanings below
decks.

'How is we going to get a
mermaid?' hissed Polly Roger, a girl
pirate with a pink parrot.

'*Where* is we going to get one

from?' whispered Fred
Bilge, who cleaned out
the toilets.

Unable to sleep a wink for worry
and the threat of Belching Bessy,
the crew huffed and puffed and
hummed and ah-haaed. From the
deck above came the ragged voice
of the captain.

'Call that supper?' he bellowed.
'You know I always has fifteen fried
eggs on my kipper! If you mess up
my food again – I'll hang you from
the highest yardarm so the seagulls

can peck out your belly buttons. Get below!'

The door to the crew's cabin flew open and two young pirates, wearing red-and-white striped tops with blue bell-bottom trousers, were hurled in. This was something that happened almost every day. Ten-

year-old twins Billy and Bobby
Briney were new to pirating and
had been press-ganged by the
captain weeks ago. They fell into a
heap, groaning, and were ignored
by the rest of the crew.

'So,' said Fred, tapping his chin,
'where will we find a mermaid?'

'I know!' said Bobby, checking
himself for bruises.

'So do I!' said Billy, checking
himself for grazes.

All eyes turned, like a shoal of
startled fish, in their direction.

Polly Roger snatched a candle and stalked over to the boys. The candlelight cast wavy shadows over their faces.

'*You* knows where to get a mermaid?' she snorted. Her pink parrot curled up its beak in disbelief.

'Saw one the other day,' said Billy softly.

'Following the ship!' said Bobby, even more softly.

Maureen and Doreen, the ocean's oldest mermaids, sat on the rudder

179

of the good ship *Weevil* combing their long grey hair and gazing at their reflections in the calm sea. The moonlight was glinting off the surface of the water when suddenly Maureen squawked, 'This eye-liner's running again!'

'You should try water-resistant!' said Doreen, touching up her lipstick.

'Oh, what's the use? I've tried it all – bubble baths, bath salts, gels, deodorant, lipstick,

180

lip gloss, rouge and blusher and I still can't find a merman to marry!'

Doreen sighed. 'I know. We trawl ocean after ocean looking for someone tall, dark and handsome but we only ever meet unwashed pirates with grizzly beards and breath like mouldy haddock!'

At that point there was a very loud splash followed by a gurgle and a spluttering. Doreen and Maureen shrieked and looked down into the dark waters below. Something had fallen from the ship

181

and plopped under the surface.
As they gazed down, a hairy
face began to emerge from the
waves, smiling a toothless grin at
the mermaids. The face and chest
belonged to Fred Bilge but his lower
half was not what he usually carried
with him. It was made entirely of
scales and fins.

Maureen and Doreen eyed
him suspiciously, before clutching
each other and squawking, 'It's a
merman!'

Suddenly there was another splash

182

and another splosh and another plop. Maureen and Doreen looked up. 'It's raining mermen!' they chorused in amazement.

Once Billy and Bobby Briny had made their announcement, the pirates had launched themselves into action. They'd decided to disguise themselves as mermen to lure the mermaids aboard. It seemed a simple plan, but these were simple pirates. The ship had been awash with scurrying and scuttling as

they'd ransacked every cubbyhole
and grubby hold for material. Fred
Bilge tore his hammock from its
moorings and tossed it across his
tummy.

'Look!' he said. 'Scales!'

Polly Roger madly
cut up a leather
jerkin to make fins.
Snippings flew
everywhere.

In a frantic
flurry of
activity, each pirate

fashioned themself a costume – some ripped apart disused sails, some carefully sewed beer mats together, some formed tails from old pillowcases.

'Stop!' bellowed Fred. 'What about the colours? What colour are merfolk?'

The pirates stopped stitching, ripping and forming.

'The ones we saw were mainly green!' piped up Billy.

'Green it will be – crack open a keg of paint!'

And so the pirates began sloshing dollops of green paint across their hastily made costumes. Many had taken so much to the idea they began splashing themselves with exotic perfumes and some even cut their hair . . .

'It's raining mermen!' shrieked Maureen and Doreen again, as pirate after pirate plopped into the bubbling blue sea.

'Hello,' said Maureen nervously. 'Thanks for dropping in!'

186

Fred Bilge was the first of the bobbing pirates to gather his wits.

'We is mermen – just look at our flappy tails – and we was a-gazing upon your beautiful faces from afar!'

'How far?'

'That far!' he said, pointing to the deck of the ship. 'And we decided to throw ourselves at your tails and declare our love!'

'Love?' said Maureen, with a sniff of suspicion.

'Love?' said Doreen, with a whiff of derision.

'Yes. Love – L . . . U . . . V . . .
and we was a-wondering whether
you lovely mermaids would like to
come aboard this here ship and be
treated like queens!'

The mermaids were going to take
a lot more convincing than that.

Treading water and hiding behind
her new false beard, Polly Roger
grabbed Fred Bilge by the ear and
whispered:

'Persuade them!'

'How?'

'Say something soft and sweet!'

188

So Fred turned to the waiting mermaids, winked broadly and said, 'Chocolate fudge!'

Maureen and Doreen looked at each other and then back at the bobbing faces below them.

'Well, all right, we'll come aboard – but only for a while. We start to wither if we stay out of water long,' explained Doreen.

"Tis not a problem, my ladies. We have aboard this ship the finest bathtub ever to grace the ocean. There is room for at least three or

189

four beautiful ladies of your build!'

Doreen and Maureen looked at their build and thought it must be a very big bathtub, indeed. Finally, Doreen said, 'Very well, haul us aboard, boys!'

It took an awful lot of rope and an awful lot of tugging to finally land the mermaids on deck. They were then carried and plopped into the bathtub with a great deal of splashing. Captain Copperknuckle, who'd been in the land of Nod while all this madness had occurred, wasn't pleased.

'What is all this noise, boys?' he snarled, rubbing his eyes as the costumed crew came into focus. 'And why are you dressed as fish?'

'Fish?' asked Maureen.

'These are mermen!' followed Doreen. 'And hunky examples too!' she added, throwing a broad wink at Polly Roger, who gulped slightly. So did her pink parrot.

Captain Copperknuckle giggled then the giggle became a chortle

171

and the chortle turned into a guffaw and the guffaw ended up as a hoot.

'Mermen? Them? You're way off the mark, you are! They're nothing but a pongy throng of pirates! But at least they finally found me some mermaids.' And the captain laughed some more and splattered the room with apple pips.

As he laughed, the pirates removed their disguises. The fins flopped to the floor and the scales fell from their knees.

Maureen and Doreen clutched each other in alarm and then screamed:

'We've been diddled!'

'Fiddled!'

'Swizzled!'

'Swindled!'

'Cheated!'

193

'Nobbled!'

'And conned!'

Doreen threw the rubber duck at the captain. The *ber-doing* it made as it bounced off his head was lost in a tidal wave of laughter.

The next morning all was still aboard the *Weevil* – not a crab was stirring. All that could be heard was the occasional snore of the pirates as they slept off the effects of last night's celebration. Captain Copperknuckle had thrown open

194

his drinks cabinet and unleashed
his kazoo-playing on the crew, and
they had slurped and burped and
danced and pranced into the early
hours. Now Billy and Bobby Briny
were the only ones awake – having
been left out of the celebrations,
they leaped out of their hammock
bright and breezy, ready to face the
day. But just as they were cracking
open their breakfast eggs they heard
a strange wailing sound. They were
drawn towards it as if enchanted,
leaving their eggs sizzling in the

175

pan. They followed it through the wooden doors of the ship, up, up the squeaky wooden steps towards the cabin of Captain Copperknuckle. And, as they drew nearer, the sound got louder and louder.

Billy and Bobby threw open the door and saw Doreen and Maureen in the bathtub.

'Maureen's got her tail-fin stuck in the plughole!' shouted Doreen. 'And she's wailing in pain!'

'Oooooooooooooooooooooooooooo ooooooooooooo!' went Maureen.

Bobby leaped over to Maureen and started tugging at her fin.

'It's no use!'

Billy grabbed her under the armpits and pulled and pulled and pulled until, with one final yank, she popped free. Bobby hurriedly replaced the plug, and all four let out a sigh of relief.

Maureen and Doreen sat in the cold bathwater and Bobby and Billy sat on the edge of the bath, wondering what to say.

'What were you doing?' asked Bobby eventually.

'Trying to escape,' explained Maureen. 'We can't spend the rest of our lives in a bathtub. We were diddled into being here. We're mermaids – we're supposed to splash free across the ocean waves!'

Doreen added, 'I told her she'd never fit down the plughole, but she wouldn't listen!'

'Can't you do something to help us?' pleaded Maureen.

Bobby placed his hand on Billy's

178

shoulder and drew him to one side. They huddled together and began to whisper soft and low.

'A plan is a-hatching, Maureen. Mark my words!' said Doreen, tapping her nose.

Billy and Bobby shook hands with each other, nodded solemnly and returned.

'We've got a plan,' said Billy.

'Ha! Told you!' shrieked Doreen, slapping the water and splashing Maureen.

'Like you, my brother and I no

199

longer wish to be aboard this boat. We are treated roughly by the captain and many of the crew, and we too wish to be free!'

Bobby and Billy moved closer to the mermaids, looked about to make sure no one was listening and began to explain their plan.

Below decks, Captain Copperknuckle was stalking the hammock room, prodding the crew with his wooden leg.

He had two fine sea legs of his own, but he found this wooden leg washed up on a beach, claimed it for himself and so he used it to prod people.

'Awaken, you salty sea dogs' – prod prod – 'and set about your tasks. The sail needs a-trimming, the compass needs a-boxing and my breakfast needs a-frying!'

The snoring sailors hiccupped and snorted, but didn't wake.

'So you's refusing to awaken.

201

Well, I think it's time for the hosepipe, my lads!'

Back in the captain's cabin, the plan had been explained. Doreen had whipped the plug from the plughole and Billy and Bobby Briny were on their knees, spannering free the bolts that held the tub to the planks below. Just as the final drop of water disappeared down the plughole, the last bolt came loose and Maureen put the plug back in.

'Right!' said Billy. 'Over to the window!'

And with a huge effort Billy and Bobby began inching the loaded bathtub towards the window, its rusty legs scratching and scraping deep grooves into the wood.

Maureen and Doreen giggled with delight as they gazed through the floor-to-ceiling window at the vast ocean before them.

'Break the window!' ordered Bobby.

'With what?' asked Maureen.

At that point Captain Copperknuckle came stomping into his cabin  looking for his hosepipe and threw his wooden leg on his desk with a clatter. He froze at the sight before him.

'What in the blithering of blue blazes is you a-doing with my bathtub and why is that mermaid trying to break that window with my rubber duck?' he yelled.

The twins threw each other a nod and sprang into action. Billy grabbed the captain's black beard and began twirling him around by it. Bobby grabbed the wooden leg and hurled it over to Maureen and Doreen.

'Use this to break the window!' he commanded.

Once every shard of glass had been smashed from its place, a glaring, gaping hole emerged – just about the size of a bathtub.

Billy was still twirling the giddy captain when his brother yelled, 'Drop him now and help me push!'

205

So they pushed the bathtub towards the broken window and the open sea below.

A very dizzy Captain Copperknuckle clutched at his desk and managed to catch a final glimpse of his bathtub, now carrying Billy and Bobby as well as the mermaids, as it tottered on the edge of the window for a split second before finally plunging into the waves below.

Chryssie in the Drywrld

Fiona Dunbar

'. . . In their world, they call their surface the *skie*,' said Miss Pearl. 'Everybody together . . . *skie*.'

'SKIE,' repeated the class.

'Please, miss, is that the top of the stuff called yair?' asked Chryssie.

'That's right,' said Miss Pearl.

'And in this yair swim creatures called bards and pleens. Etch that on your shell.'

Chryssie scratched eagerly away with her stone stylus on her giant clamshell. She loved learning about the Dryworld; she could barely wait for the Face of the Surf Ceremony, when she would finally venture up there with the rest of the ten-year-olds for the very first time. No one was *ever* allowed up before they turned ten.

'I heard that pleens swallow

huge numbers of humans!' babbled
Mara Roe, looping the loop like
a crazed shrimp. 'Then they swim
far away, and spit them out again
– completely whole!'

This caused much excited
discussion.

'Quiet!' called Miss Pearl.
'Everyone's heard such tales, Mara.
But it has never been proven. These
pleens are similar to *chips*, like the
one whose skeleton lies the other
side of Spirogyra.'

Chryssie knew this chip well; it

was called the *Titanic*, and she and
her friends had spent many a long
hour playing around its skeleton.

'And, as we know, chips are quite
safe for humans,' Miss Pearl went
on, 'until they die, and sink. So the
humans die too, because . . . ?'

'Because they haven't got gills
like us?' suggested Lila Lin.

'That's right, Lila,' said Miss
Pearl. 'Without gills, they can't
breathe underwater.'

'But *we* can breathe in the yair,'
said Chryssie.

'Well, yes,' said Miss Pearl. 'As long as you're qualified. But I believe you've now completed your yair-breathing training, is that right?'

'Yes!' cried the class, proudly waving their scallop-shell medals. They had practised using yair-filled vessels, and now they were almost ready for the ceremony. The excitement was almost too much to bear; ten whole years they had waited for this!

'Excellent. But remember:

no going up to the Dryworld unaccompanied, all right?'

'Yes, Miss Pearl,' mumbled the mermaids.

'Good girls.' Miss Pearl swam down from her coral seat. 'Now, to come back to the skie. It's very important that you—'

At that moment, a loud horn echoed around the class, and everyone groaned. It was a volcano alert; it meant that Old Barun was about to blow. 'I'm sorry,' said Miss Pearl abruptly, 'but we'll have to stop the lesson now.'

There was uproar. 'But, Miss Pearl!' protested Chryssie. 'We *must* finish, or we won't learn everything in time for tomorrow's ceremony!' Everyone agreed. No one was worried about the alert; they got them all the time, and usually the underwater volcano only quivered and spluttered a bit, then calmed down.

Miss Pearl swished around, waving them on. 'There may be no ceremony! Now come along!'

213

The mermaids packed their shells on their backs and headed for the safety cave as the horn sounded once again. 'Hey, Chryssie,' said Lila. 'Don't look so glum – it might still happen.'

'But I bet it won't,' said Chryssie. 'And we've been looking forward to this moment all our lives!'

'Yeah, and then *you'll* have to wait till the next neap tide,' snorted Mara Roe. 'But *I* won't, 'cause I've got a rich dad. I'll get a special fast-track ceremony, and I'll only have to wait a *day*. Ha ha!'

'Clam up, Mara!' snapped Lila, and she and Chryssie spurted away from her.

'Ooh, I could just set the lobsters on to that girl!' fumed Chryssie.

'Her parents are such show-offs,' remarked Lila. 'They couldn't care less about local traditions.'

Old Gasper the turtle sailed by. 'Hurry up, girls, no dawdling! The eruption's already ruined the stadium!'

215

'The *stadium*?' Chryssie and Lila looked at each other; they knew exactly what this meant. 'So the Face of the Surf Ceremony . . . ?'

Old Gasper shook his head. 'Oh, definitely cancelled.'

'So it'll have to wait until the next neap tide?' asked Chryssie.

'Maybe until the one after that,' said Old Gasper. The horn sounded again. 'Come along, quickly!'

Next neap tide – or maybe the one after that! That was ages away,

216

at least forty days. 'Come along, Chryssie,' said Lila. 'There's nothing we can do about it.'

But Chryssie had already made up her mind that there *was* something she could do about it . . .

Chryssie waited in the cave with everyone else until a messenger declared there had been no further damage in Spirogyra, and it was safe to return. Then, as the mer-people began happily spilling out of the caves, she slipped away. Flipping her tail with all her strength, she rose higher and higher. Nobody noticed; they were all so eager to get back to their homes.

I will *see the skie!* Chryssie thought, propelling herself upwards. Ten years was quite long enough; she couldn't bear to wait any longer. She'd heard it was blue, but not like sea blue – much brighter, they'd said. Luminous, like the light the squid and the anglerfish sometimes gave off in the darkest depths of the ocean.

Chryssie gazed down. The water was misty from the eruption, and soon she could see nobody. She felt a shiver of excitement. Never before had she been so completely alone. It was a scary feeling – but thrilling too.

Higher and higher . . . then, after what felt like an age, a rush of warmer water told her she was nearing the top.

She trembled, despite the warmth. Would she manage the yair-breathing? 'Close your gills,' she told

herself, 'suck in the yair through

your nose or mouth, then blow it

out again.' What would it feel like?

Dry . . . whatever that meant.

Golden ripples appeared above

her. She reached up her hand,

and it slid into . . . something else.

Warmer, she supposed, and lighter.

Closing her gills, she shot upwards, eyes scrunched shut.

But when she opened her eyes the skie was nothing like she had expected at all.

There was a big round orange thing. And the skie wasn't blue, but red and yellow and coral pink . . . and there were puffy greyish things all around that were edged in orange as well. The skie was exploding, like a volcano!

No, it can't be, Chryssie thought. Perhaps she wasn't seeing right

221

– maybe her eyes needed to adjust to the yair as well. She pulled herself up on to some nearby rocks and thought hard about what it might be, but it was no use. She would definitely have remembered anything about a giant orange ball in the skie! And it seemed to be moving; she was sure it was lower now than when she'd first seen it. And the puffy grey things seemed to have grown redder. Chryssie looked around for any bards or pleens to ask, but the only bards she could see were too far away, and there weren't any pleens. Which was just as well – what if one came and swallowed her up, like it did with humans? She might never find her way home.

Now the skie was burning furiously, and the orange thing seemed larger . . . and lower!

'Oh my!' gasped Chryssie. 'It's heading for the sea!' Never mind Old Barun – now the whole ocean was in danger. She would have to warn everyone, right away!

Chryssie plunged back into the waves, her mind reeling. *There'll be adults who'll know what to do,* she thought. *Perhaps something like this has happened before . . . but they'll need warning.*

Down and down she went, through shoal after shoal of shimmering fishes, until at last the domes and spires of Spirogyra appeared below.

First she came to Old Gasper, who had been out searching for her.

'Oh, Gasper, something terrible's about to happen!' she told him.

Miss Pearl hurried to join them. 'What is it, Chryssie?'

Others, too, gathered around. Neighbours popped their heads up through their homeholes. 'Something terrible?' they muttered. 'What is it?'

'I . . . I went up to the surface, and—'

'The surface? She went up to the surface?' muttered the neighbours. 'How old is she? Is she qualified?' went the chatter, on and on from

225

one Spirogyra homehole to the
next.

'I know, I know I wasn't
supposed to,' cried Chryssie, as loud
as she could, 'but I couldn't wait,
and . . . well, it's just as well that
I did, because there's some sort of
fireball ripping through the
skie, and it's heading for
the ocean!'

'A fireball?' said Miss Pearl.

'Yes! It's huge and orange, and
it's already ripped the skie to shreds!'

'When you say "ripped the skie

226

to shreds",' said Miss Pearl, 'what *exactly* did you see?'

'Well, there were these sort of puffy greyish-orange bits . . .' She trailed off, trying to read Miss Pearl's expression.

'Chryssie, you haven't learned about *klowds* yet, have you?' said Miss Pearl.

'Um . . .'

'Or a setsun . . .'

'Well, I—'

There were murmurings all around. Chryssie felt her cheeks burn

227

as she began to realize she'd made a complete clownfish of herself.

'Chryssie,' said Miss Pearl, 'there's a reason why you have to finish your course before going up to the surface. If you had, you would have learned that the sun – the orange thing you saw – burns the skie *every* night. This turns the skie black, but you can see the millions of tiny holes in it from all the burnings.

But it never tears or breaks; it is very strong.' She smiled kindly.

'Poor Chryssie.

228

You have had a shock, haven't you?'

Chryssie wanted to bury herself in the sand – never had she been so embarrassed!

The next day at school, Mara Roe started teasing straight away. 'So, *Chryssie*, isn't it amazing that we're all still here after that ball of fire plunged into the sea? Hee hee hee!'

Chryssie's cheeks were aflame again. 'Well . . .' she trailed off.

But then Lila Lin and a gaggle

229

of friends shimmied over. 'Ooh, Chryssie! Tell us all about it! What was it like?'

Everyone huddled around her. 'Was it hard to breathe?' 'What does a setsun look like?' 'Did you see any bards or pleens?'

They had quite
forgotten Chryssie's
embarrassing mistake;
all they wanted were
the details of her adventure. So
Chryssie told them, soon relishing
the memory of her horror when she
had thought her world was about
to come to an end, and describing a
skie aglow with fire.

Mara Roe slithered off alone;
nobody was interested in teasing
Chryssie, after all. Worse, *she* would
no longer be the centre of attention

after her exclusive Face of the Surf ceremony.

Chryssie almost felt sorry for her – almost, but not quite. After all, Mara would see the skie herself the very next day, while Chryssie would have to wait for the next neap tide, or the one after that. No matter. She could cherish the memory of that glorious setsun until then . . .

The Mermaid Who Came to School

Moira Munro

When Leena was lonely – which
was most of the time because
her parents worked all day
on their oyster farm – she
practised walking on the bottom
of the sea. Swinging from
side to side on the very tip

of her fish tail, she played at being a human.

In the mornings, as soon as her mum and dad had left to check the oysters for pearls, she sneaked away to the shore. She hid in the waves that lapped against the sea wall, looking up at the little school just above.

What I'd like to do, she thought, watching the chattering children who gathered by the school gates, *what I'd really like to do, is get up on that jetty and join them.* When she was

little Grandma had told her tales
of mermaids making friends with
humans. It was rumoured that her
great-great-aunt had run off, as a
young mermaid, to marry a man.
Dad snorted at these stories. 'Sea
spray and nonsense! Never forget,
Leena, that humans are worse than
sharks.'

But there was one girl her age,
Megan, whom Leena especially
liked. Every morning before school,
Megan skipped down to the beach
for an early swim with her mother.

235

Megan was a big smiler. Even when she shrieked that the water was freezing her toes she never stopped smiling. What's more, she swam almost as well as a mermaid. Leena dipped and dived around her, quick as a mackerel, so that Megan would not see her.

But, last week, her father had caught her by the shore and sent her straight back into the deep.

'Are you mad, Leena?'

'But, Dad, I have nothing to do! I don't even have any friends.'

He'd ruffled her hair. 'I wish we could live closer to a school, Leena. But this is where the farm is. I'm sorry.'

All week, Leena had stayed away from the shore, but, as she tossed about in the raging sea, the wind constantly whisked her mind off towards the little school.

Finally, one blustery morning, Leena could stand it no longer. With a determined flip of her tail, she sped

towards the shore. If she hurried, she would be in time to see the children coming into school.

She didn't expect to see the purple dragon in front of the gates. For a wild moment, Leena wondered if she'd been sucked into one of Grandma's tales. As she rubbed her eyes, two giggling princesses and an alien joined the dragon and chased it into the school. Leena noticed a banner hung above the entrance, with the words WORLD BOOK DAY on it.

Wow! Leena thought. *They're all dressed up as storybook characters.*

Megan arrived just as the bell was ringing. She wore a shimmery top, a sparkling necklace, and – Leena's heart skipped a beat – a glossy fishtail that went right down to her ankles. Leena danced a little jig in the sea. Of all the possible characters Megan could have picked, she'd chosen to be a mermaid.

An idea began to form in Leena's mind. It was a crazy idea. It was dangerous. If her parents ever found

out, they'd never let her out of their
sight again. She'd be stuck with
them at the farm, twiddling her
flipper while they tended the oysters,
or worse: they'd put her on pearl-
stringing duties. But, she thought
with a leap of her heart, it's now or
never.

Ten minutes later, Megan was
walking through the school corridor
with a message for the Head, her
fishtail flapping around her ankles.
Megan loved her costume. Often,

in the sea, she glimpsed flashes
of rainbow and fancied that a
mysterious mermaid was playing
hide-and-seek with her. Megan
dipped her head and pressed her
palms together. She was gliding in
the water currents. She was leaping
in the foam. There, just beyond the
corner, she would join the biggest
wave that—

THUMP!

Megan flung her arms out to
steady herself. Her hands caught
another pair of hands. Delicate

hands, cool and slightly damp.

Megan looked down in amazement.

The girl she'd bumped into was also

dressed as a mermaid. How beautiful

she was, with her big eyes and her sleek hair, so shiny she could have come straight out of the sea. And how her fish tail shimmered!

The two girls grinned at each other. Leena clung on to Megan's hands, trying to recover her balance. She might have practised walking on the seabed for hours, but doing it on dry land was much more difficult.

Megan held her steady, laughing. 'These fish tails are terrible! I keep falling over as well. It's cool how your tail completely hides your feet!'

Leena giggled. 'That's because mine's real!'

She instantly wished she could take back her words. 'Don't listen to me – I'm just pulling your fin.'

But Megan wasn't paying attention anyway. 'Where did you get your costume?' she gushed. 'Mine's from Toy World. Your necklace is awesome. I bought one like that at the One Pound Shop, but it's not so pearly.'

'Have it if you like,' Leena said, handing it over. There were plenty more pearls at the farm. They were nothing special to her, nothing as special as a friend. Megan unclasped her own string of glass beads and hooked it round Leena's neck.

'You look lost – are you new? I'll take you to see the Head.'

She led the way, joking that Miss Turner would be amazed to see two mermaids at once.

A big black dog leaped up from behind the Head's desk the instant the girls entered the office. He

245

growled and snapped at Leena's tail.
Miss Turner jumped from her chair
and yanked him away.

'Sit, Duke, *sit!*' she cried. 'What on
earth's the matter with you?'

'He thinks Leena's costume is
dinner!' Megan joked.

When Miss Turner realized that
Leena had come in without her
parents, she became most flustered.

'Let me get this clear,' she said.
'Your parents just dropped you off?
Without coming to see me?'

Leena had been taught not to tell

246

lies. 'I, er, came on my own, Miss Turner.'

'You walked from home, all by yourself?'

'Walked? Hmm . . . not exactly.'

Miss Turner frowned. 'Where are your parents?'

'Oh, they're busy on the farm.'

Miss Turner returned to her desk. She had a slight limp, Leena noticed.

'Listen,' Miss Turner said gently, 'however busy your parents are, they need to come in right away, and either register you properly or

247

take you home. What's their phone number?'

Leena's eyes searched the ceiling. Foam number? What was that all about?

Miss Turner continued. 'Leena, where do you live?'

Leena's face lit up. 'The ocean.'

'Ocean Avenue,' Miss Turner said. 'Hallelujah, we're getting somewhere. What number?'

Leena bit her lip. She didn't know oceans had numbers.

Miss Turner sank in her chair.

'So, no phone number, no address . . .'

For a while, the only sound was the drumming of her fingers on the desk. Megan gave Leena's hand a little squeeze.

Finally, Miss Turner stood up.

'Leena, I need time to look into this,' she said. 'Meanwhile, you'd better stay with us, where at least you'll be safe.'

Leena beamed, relieved. Never mind that tomorrow World Book Day would be over, and she would have to go back to her own world. Today, while everyone was dressed up, she would have a wonderful time pretending to be a child. A child dressed up as a mermaid.

The children in Megan's class gazed, open-mouthed, at the beautiful new girl.

'I'm asking everyone to talk about their storybook character,' said the teacher, Mr Brown. 'Trandulah, it's your turn. Why are you disguised as a fairy?'

250

'So we can't see she's a witch!' shouted one of the boys.

Trandulah scowled at him. 'See my magic wand? When I wave it everyone has to do what I say.'

'And if they don't,' a girl sniggered, 'Tell-Tale Trandulah will tell the teacher, as usual!'

The class giggled.

'That's enough, everyone,' Mr Brown said. 'Now, would our two mermaids like to explain their characters?'

'Mermaids are beautiful,'

251

Megan began. Leena nodded enthusiastically, grinning.

'We're awesome swimmers,' Megan added.

Leena agreed. 'We can swim in the wildest of seas.'

'And we're mysterious,' Megan continued. 'We sit on rocks with our sisters and comb our silken hair.'

'Not me,' Leena interrupted, rolling her eyes. 'I don't have any sisters. There are no other mermaid children for miles, and no mermaid school. I sit on my own at the bottom of the sea, getting bored out of my fish tail, while my mum and dad work on their oyster farm.'

Everyone laughed.

'But we don't mind having nothing to do,' Megan said, 'because we get to keep an eye out for handsome princes who need rescuing.'

Leena screwed up her nose. 'With my luck, my prince would be as ugly as a sea snail.'

The class burst into laughter again.

253

'For the sake of love,' Megan continued, 'we will gladly give up our enchanting voices, like the little mermaid did in the story. It's supposed to be a beautiful and brave thing to do.'

'I'd never be so stupid,' Leena said. 'What if, after all that trouble, my prince picked his nose at the table? I wouldn't even have a voice to yell at him!'

Mr Brown chuckled. 'All right, thank you, mermaids. Now, for those of you who'd like to perform

254

in the school musical, Miss Turner
and I will audition you now.'

Megan grasped Leena's arm.
'They're only going to choose the
best singers,' she whispered. 'I'm so
nervous.'

Leena smiled. 'Don't be.
Remember, you're a mermaid today.
Mermaids have beautiful voices.' She
nudged Megan. 'Unless they lose
them for a daft prince!'

As Megan sang her audition piece,
she imagined she was a mermaid
gliding through the seas. Miss Turner

255

and Mr Brown beamed at her. 'Well done! You're in,' they said.

But when it was Leena's turn to sing – a lilting, otherworldly melody – a hush fell over the room. Never before had anybody heard anything so pure, so sweet, so perfect. When Leena stopped, there was a long silence. Then somebody clapped, and the class broke out in cheers.

'Leena,' Miss Turner said, wiping her eyes, 'even a real mermaid couldn't sing more enchantingly.'

Trandulah fiddled with her fairy

256

wand, scowling. She hadn't been chosen.

At lunchtime, Megan and Leena made their way to the dining hall together, followed by a dozen other girls who all wanted to sit with Leena.

'I'm so hungry,' Leena said.

'You *look* hungry,' Megan said, putting her arm round her. 'You're not even walking straight. Unless it's your costume that's too tight.'

Trandulah was

ahead of them in the queue. 'Fish fingers,' she ordered.

Leena stared in horror. Her tail went weak and wobbly, forcing Megan to steady her.

'Don't you like fish?' Megan asked.

'I do,' Leena said. 'They don't say much, but they're very friendly.'

Megan burst out laughing. 'Sounds like you'd better have the veggie dish.'

When the dinner lady held out her hand for money, Leena opened

a little pearl bag and scooped
out a handful of battered
silver coins.

The dinner lady chuckled. 'I see
you're a proper little mermaid! Let
me guess – is this ancient treasure
from a sunken ship? Now darling,
I'd prefer some real money, if you
don't mind.'

Megan wondered what kind of a
strange life Leena had if her parents
could send her to a new school
alone without even giving her lunch
money. She pushed a coin into

259

Leena's hand, saying, 'Have it. I'm not that hungry myself.'

'We'll share,' Leena said.

Trandulah swivelled round. 'We're not allowed to give away our lunch money,' she whined. 'I'm going to tell Miss Turner. And stop laughing, or you'll be in big trouble.'

In the afternoon, Mr Brown talked to them about the stars, some of which are so far away that the light coming from them has taken millions of years to travel to us. Leena wished she could listen to him forever. Nobody, not even Grandma, had ever told her about stars. And nobody had ever asked her to perform in a musical and nobody had ever laughed with her and exchanged necklaces. As the last bell of the day rang, her heart sank to the bottom of her tail. This was it, then. Time to return to the sea.

A fierce wind was blowing in, and rain lashed Leena and Megan's faces as they made their way out of the front door. Children barged past them to race down the steps,

covering their heads with their
school bags. Megan watched
thoughtfully as Leena wobbled down
the wheelchair ramp, her fingers
gripping the wet handrail, and
perched herself on a bench by the
sea wall. Why did Leena look so
sad?

Megan fingered the necklace
Leena had given her.

Suddenly, it all made sense.

Leena's strange coins, her
reaction to the fish
fingers, her beautiful

voice and, of course, the rainbow
fish tail that mysteriously hid her
feet.

'You're a real mermaid!' she cried.

Leena looked up in alarm. A huge
wave crashed below them, showering
them with spray.

'But you are coming back
tomorrow, aren't you?' Megan
shouted above the storm.

Leena swiped at her tail. 'The
school uniform's hardly going to
hide *this*.'

'Tell Miss Turner the truth,'

Megan cried. 'She won't mind. As long as your parents come to register you.'

Leena shook her head. 'Humans are dangerous – not you, of course, but other people. Mermaids never come on to dry land; it's not like in stories! I only risked it today because everyone was in disguise.'

Megan glared at her. 'You're not even trying.'

She took Megan's hand. 'I swim with you every morning, you know. We can still be mermaid sisters.'

264

'That's not good enough. I thought we were best friends.'

'You don't understand,' Leena cried. 'I can never, ever let people know I'm a mermaid!'

'I heard that,' interrupted a shrill voice. Megan and Leena swivelled round to see Trandulah just behind them. 'You're half *fish*!' she shrieked.

She skipped round the bench and plonked herself on the rail at the edge of the sea wall. 'Hey, everyone,' she shouted, waving her wand high in the air, 'over here!'

265

'Get off the rail!' warned Megan.

'I'll tell the cook so she can turn you into fish fingers!'

Trandulah's mother charged towards them. 'TRANDULAH!' she screamed. 'Come away from the edge!'

Trandulah ignored her. 'And I'll tell Miss Turner,' she shouted, throwing her arms up in the air. 'She'll have a fit if she finds out a sea creature was in her school.'

'TRANDULAH!' Megan and Leena leaped up, but it was too

266

late. Trandulah overbalanced and fell backwards over the edge of the wall. Trandulah's mother reached them just in time to see a huge wave carrying her daughter away. For a few seconds there was chaos. Parents, children, Miss Turner, were screaming all at once. Some people wanted to jump into the raging sea, while others held them back.

The next instant, everyone gasped as a girl with a rainbow fish tail leaped off the wall. They watched her glide smoothly through the wild waters towards Trandulah.

'That's Leena,' they shouted. 'Look! She's a real mermaid.'

'She's gorgeous!'

A few minutes later, Leena returned the spluttering Trandulah to the jetty, and a great cheer rose from the crowd. Trandulah burst into tears in her mother's arms.

Miss Turner held her hands out to Leena. 'Why didn't you tell me?' she cried. She held Leena tight. 'Did you think I'd turn you away?'

The children crowded around Leena, hugging her. Trandulah's mother ran over and planted a kiss on her cheek, before rushing away with her shivering daughter. Suddenly everyone realized how wet they were and ran off home to get dried off.

'Goodbye, Leena,' Miss Turner said. 'I'll see you in school tomorrow.'

'I can't . . .' Leena spluttered.

'My parents won't ever . . .' The storm drowned her voice out, but Miss Turner understood.

'Ask them to meet me. I'll come here myself tomorrow, at sunrise.'

'But, Miss Turner, you're . . .' How could she say this politely? '. . . not a mermaid, and my mum and dad would never trust—'

'I know,' Miss Turner said.

She bent down and tugged at the zip on her boot. Leena and Megan

270

watched her, puzzled. Hopping on one leg, Miss Turner pulled her boot off, and then her sock.

Instead of a big toe, Miss Turner had a small, rainbow-coloured fin.

'Wow!' said Leena.

'Awesome!' said Megan.

Miss Turner smiled. 'Tell your parents that my great-great-grandmother lived at Ocean Avenue too!' Then she put her sock on, zipped up her boot and walked back to the school gates.

Megan clapped her hands.

271

'Problem solved. She's practically a member of your family.'

'What's Dad going to say to that!' laughed Leena.

'Whatever he says, Miss Turner never takes no for an answer,' said Megan.

'Then you'll see me in school tomorrow!'

Megan threw herself forward to hug her, and Leena lost her balance and they tumbled, shrieking, into a puddle, but as they were both wet anyway, it just made them laugh even more.

'By the way,' Megan said, 'it was good of you to rescue Trandulah. It was horrible when she fell in. Even though she is a pain.'

'I really didn't want to jump in,' Leena said. 'Not with everyone watching.'

'You risked everything for a human being – if you can call Trandulah that. Like the little mermaid did for her prince.'

273

'Ahem!' Leena grinned. 'There is still one very big difference.'

'Oh yes?' Megan said. 'And what might that be?'

'The difference, mermaid sister, is . . .'

'Yes?' Megan said.

'That I would never, ever be so soppy as to rescue a prince.'

The Mermaid and the Song

Anna Wilson

A retelling of the traditional Cornish folktale,
'The Mermaid of Zennor'

Morven closed her eyes. That music
again!

She lay back on her bed of
seaweed and smiled, drinking in
the silvery notes that drifted out
from across the bay,
over the ocean's

surface, weaving their way down,

down into her watery cave.

Six moons had come and gone

since the first time Morven had

heard the voice.

'Who is it that sings those melodies?' she whispered to herself.

She swam to the mouth of the cavern and tilted her smooth, oval face up towards the sea's ceiling. So transported was she by the music that she let herself float upwards, her eyes still closed. Nothing would come between her and this haunting song.

'What now, dreamer?' snapped Demelza angrily. In her distracted state, Morven had drifted straight into her older sister and knocked a

277

shell mirror out of her hands. The mirror fell to the ocean's bed and landed on a coral reef, where it shattered into myriad pieces.

Demelza shrieked with rage and lashed out at her sister with her tail. 'You awkward barnacle!'

Morven darted to one side, avoiding her sister's thrashing fins, and glowered at Demelza. The older mermaid always appeared at the wrong time, in the wrong place. One look from her piercing green eyes and even the calmest wave ruffled in fear.

'Your reflection would have shattered the glass in an instant,' Morven muttered. It was not in her nature to be unkind, but the mere mention of Demelza's name was often enough to stir up a bitter taste in her mouth.

Demelza's eyes narrowed, as if considering what punishment her sister's insolence deserved, but her attention was caught by the bewitching tune. 'Such a raucous

racket!' she scowled, knitting her
dark eyebrows together. 'Those
humans whining and howling again,
I suppose. It makes my scales stand
on end.'

Morven bristled anew at her
sister's insensitivity.

'Racket?' she said. 'How can you
be so brutal? You are jealous, that
is all.' Seeing the look of outrage on
her sister's dull features, she felt the
cruel satisfaction that comes from
rubbing salt into another's open
wound.

'Oh, so you think a man can sing better than a mermaid?' Demelza sniped. 'You simple little fish—'

She stopped abruptly, her dour face brightening for an instant as she realized the true effect of the music on her little sister's soul. 'But wait – no, it can't be true . . .' She feigned great surprise and put a hand up to her cheek. 'Has my little sister fallen in love – with a *human being*?'

Morven felt her blood run hot. 'And what if I have?' she retorted, lifting her pretty chin high in a poor attempt at hiding her feelings.

Demelza cackled nastily and swished deeper into the ocean's darkness. 'Your story will end in salty tears, sister,' she crowed. 'You mark my words!'

Deep in her heart, Morven feared her sister was right. Mermaids had no business mixing with creatures of the land. But that voice! It was low and smooth: as sonorous as the song of the whales, and yet more powerful. She had to know to whom it belonged. And she was scared — for what would happen to her if she left her seabed and went to walk among men? The myths of the sea told the sorry tales of mermaids who had tried to live on the land — their scales dried out, their hair turned to crisp seaweed, their beauty perished as a seashell loses its bloom when it is left too

283

long out of the water. Worst of all, they were forced to walk on feet of splintered glass for all eternity. But Morven shook her golden tresses impatiently at the thought of such fairy tales.

'That's all they are – just stories,' she told herself firmly. 'No mer-creature has ever seen such a thing come to pass.' But Demelza's voice echoed in her head: 'It will all end in salty tears!'

The man's music had died away while Morven endured her sister's

284

taunts. This did not
trouble the mermaid,
however, as she had
grown accustomed to the
waxing and waning of the beautiful
sound. Although mer-creatures do
not measure time as humans do,
Morven knew by the change in the
tides that very soon she would hear
the man again.

Sure enough, one morning as
Morven swam among the dolphins
and played with the seals, the

285

music once more carried out across the bay and down into Morven's world. The mermaid determined to waste no more time in dreaming. Checking that Demelza was safely out of sight, she grabbed some shimmering sea plants with which to disguise herself and a tiny box of mother-of-pearl. With these treasures under one slender arm, she pushed with the other and thrashed her silvery tail, darting to the ocean's surface. Now that her head was above the blanket of the sea, the sound of the music was almost more than she could bear. The notes were clear, and pierced her like an arrow, straight and true into her heart.

I must follow the melody and find its maker! she thought, leaving her fears far beneath the crashing waves. But sea legends warned that should a man ever look upon the face of a mermaid, he would be bewitched and follow the creature into the sea to his death. Morven did not wish her beloved to suffer pain and die.

'It will be enough for me to catch

a glimpse of this man,' she told herself. 'I will capture the notes that rise from his throat and return to the sea where I will keep them forever in my little box.' But even as she said this her soul ached.

She reached the shore and hauled herself up out of the water. Then, hiding beneath a wooden jetty, she disguised her mermaid's body with a dazzling dress of sea shells and greenery, covering her hair and face with a shining veil of sea mist.

A tail is not designed for walking. Morven's way over the shingle beach was slow and painful, and she hobbled up the stony path into the small fishing village, following the direction of the man's voice. Once or twice she feared someone was behind her, but each time she turned to check she found that she was alone.

As she approached the village, the music grew stronger and deeper – along with the yearning in Morven's heart. She reached the proud little granite church and slipped unnoticed through the forbidding oak doors. She took a seat in an empty pew at the back, glad of the chance to rest.

Before her in the choir stalls, stood tall, dark Mathew Trewella, an ordinary miner with an extraordinary gift. Every Sunday he sang in this little church, and it was this singing that had haunted Morven for so many moons. And he was singing now – a melody that lifted the spirits of all that heard it: a golden thread of song that would stay in the heart for many days after, a musical balm to soothe the fishermen on their dark nights out at sea.

Morven fumbled with the pearly box, determined to capture the music and then return to her rightful home. But, as she did so, a hand reached out and grabbed her veil from her face. Stifling a cry, Morven struggled to replace the veil and dropped the box. The clatter rang out over the stone-flagged floor, and Mathew stopped his singing. His eyes sought out the source of the commotion. Morven, still fighting with her veil, rushed to retrieve the box and, turning, saw her sister Demelza sniggering by her side.

'Salty tears, sister!' Demelza whispered, cold menace in her eyes. 'Salty tears . . .'

Mathew was staring, still and silent as a clam.

Morven's heart tightened and she cried out in vain, 'Don't look!'

But Mathew was fixed, his eyes locked on to Morven's.

292

'Turn your gaze, mortal!' Demelza sneered. 'And come with *me*.'

The congregation called out to

Mathew. 'No, Mathew – don't go, don't look at those sea witches!'

But Mathew was unable to do as they asked. He walked slowly down the aisle until he came face to face with Morven. She trembled, waiting for her hair to shrivel into seaweed, her skin to crumble like dry sand. She closed her eyes and waited for her sister's evil magic to sweep Mathew down into the briny depths to his death. But these things did not happen. Instead Morven felt the warmth of the man's lips on